A Letter to Memphis

~

Out of Egypt Reading the King's Text

~

Nelson P. Miller

A letter to Memphis — Out of Egypt Reading the King's Text.

Miller, Nelson P.

Published by: Crown Management, LLC -- July 2014,
1527 Pineridge Drive, Grand Haven, MI 49417, USA

ISBN: 978-0-9905553-0-8

To my beloved brother,
far greater than me,
except as we share Christ.

Table of Contents

I'll be your God;
you'll be my people.

I am God, your personal God
who rescued you from Egypt
so that you would no longer
be slaves to the Egyptians.

I ripped off the harness of your slavery
so that you can move about freely.

Leviticus 26:13.

Foreword

This account is of two brothers, one alive and one lost. I leave it to you, the reader, to discern which brother is which—which alive and which lost. I fully appreciate that readers could and will disagree. As the very different lives of the two brothers well reflect, some of us pursue adventure while others of us pursue truth, while the two (adventure and truth) can be quite hard to tell apart. Perhaps it is that truth is more adventurous, making the world more immanent and authentic, than even adventure.

The brothers might be real and yet might be fictional. In another household, they could be sisters, or a parent and child. In another setting, they might be neighbors or friends, or even enemies. One, though, has written a long letter to the other. Each chapter begins with the setting in which the reader brother read the letter. The letter itself follows. Each chapter ends with an account of the writer brother's hope for the letter's impact.

The letter itself takes the form of straightforward instruction, or one might even say *exhortation*, in how to read an ancient though widely distributed text. The writer brother had found the story of that text, indeed the text's hero King, to be so transformative as to demand the attention of the literate. The writer brother wants to know that the reader brother will share that transformation. In the end, though, the letter's contents are less important than the brothers' relationship. Sometimes love just takes a good letter to connect, doesn't it?

1

Greetings

Memphis did not know that this adventure would be his last, ending like no other. He had no sense that the message he would read would be the last words of a dying man, in fact a dead man's message by the time that he finished it. If clues there had been, then he had missed them, when he was not usually one to miss clues. Yet those discoveries were yet to come. For now, the adrenaline rush that he always felt starting an adventure was still pushing him. He knew that excitement could mask things. He just didn't know yet the significance of the things he was missing.

The first quiet moment had finally arrived since well before his departure. Like each of his great trips before this one, everything had been a blur of exhausting preparations right up until the moment he had left. Then, with preparations complete and the journey begun, he had turned all of his energies to learning to navigate among the strange people, language, and culture. He had been on the great river for three full days when, finally, things had settled into a routine. His eyes had adjusted to the river scenes and sights. His ears were finally attuned to the clunking of the river boat's paddles and poles, the bird cries, and the strange sounds of the river's night. His mind had slowed enough to reflect on the events of the past few days.

A loud clunk of one of the lazy paddles against the boat's side jarred him enough to refresh his mind, as if awaking him from the dream of the frantic last preparations and embarkation. He then remembered his brother's surprise visit just before his departure. He had not seen his brother in years and not expected him to respond to his notice of this next adventure. He traveled often and returned always, giving his brother notice each time just in case his brother should try to reach him, which was unlikely except in the most urgent circumstances. He loved his brother as his brother loved him, indeed as brothers love brothers. Yet their love augured no particular fellowship. They saw one another only rarely, around life's great events like birth, marriage, and death.

That thought caused him a jolt, just as the paddle again clunked loudly against the boat. His brother had not looked well, he suddenly realized with a stab of regret for not having then noticed and said something to his brother. They had only had a rushed moment together at the station. His brother had barely caught him, with just enough time to exchange a few excited words of greeting and send-off. Then he remembered. His brother had given him a package wrapped in brown paper tied with a string, which he had quickly stowed unopened in his trunk. His brother had mentioned something about a letter that he might read on his trip. He stirred to restore blood to his seat from the river boat's hard wooden bench on which he sat. He then rose, unsteadily at first until the boat settled, to retrieve his brother's letter.

He removed the brown-paper-wrapped package from the top of the trunk where he had unceremoniously tossed and stowed it. As he did so, something stirred within him that he had not felt for a very long time, since before he could remember. It was more a feeling than a memory. He sensed its origin in a childhood event, yet one that he simply could not remember. It was so powerful that he just stood there transfixed, holding the package as the boat began to rock again unsteadily. The feeling was a little bit ominous but yet without foreboding, like the approach of something wholly positive but still so big as to be beyond important—scary but good, if that was even possible. He shook his head, breaking the spell, and made his way back to the hard wooden bench.

Greetings, Memphis, my brother and best friend. May *God look you full in the face* until you can do nothing but prosper. Judging from the high regard in which others hold you, the King must indeed reign in you, influencing you toward the good works for which your friends know you so well and creating in you the sweetness that attracts them to you. I suspect that the King has been leading you to him, that he would enthrall you for as long as you wish, indeed forever. May God *make you into what gives him most pleasure*, giving you *everything you need to please him*, even as we learn that only by pleasing him do we satisfy ourselves. Given that we find our happiness only in him, he must indeed have formed us for that highest of pursuits and purposes to move in and through him. We so draw our vitality and joy from serving him by loving others as he loved us, even lending us his authority. God grant that we know more of him by knowing more of his son the King.

This letter is only for you, Memphis, of whom I think often and whom I love deeply not only with brotherly love but also with God's love, so distinct and so much richer than human sentiment. You probably know that sometimes I write with tears and in anguish. Yet I always write out of a desire for all that I see in you that reflects my other brother the King. You are older than me, which I respect and which kept me from sharing what I have learned of him. But time runs out, and I see now that only God's spirit *makes wise human insight possible.* And so in this letter I share what I have learned about the King, that he so deeply loves you, and not just you but those whom you gather in love around you. You shine so brightly in his love. He makes your words gentle yet your hands strong and step as sure. I see in you just how rich is our King, rich in the way that he makes so much of us in the precious little time we have left here.

If I had a more diplomatic way that these words could reach you, you know that I would use it instead of this letter. You know that I wish you no trouble, not even any slight burden. Just the opposite: I have always wished you freer than you are, lighter in your step, and more joyful. I surely do not want to burden you even with a message of love. You and I should instead learn from the King his *unforced rhythms of grace* that help us live more freely and easily than seems humanly possible. You know that religion does not wear me out with heavy rules. I am the last one to urge any rules on you that would make you carry burdens that I do not carry myself.

I hope instead that you will accept this letter knowing that I wrote it in that life and Spirit to help lighten those very burdens you already carry, and not because of rules and religion but because of our condition without the King's grace. He takes the load off of us and gives us something to carry that is so light that it seems more to lift us up than to have any weight of its own. Let this letter do the same for you, which would be to lighten the load you already bear. I know it seems to both of us that our bodies and even our lives are constantly falling apart. My body falls apart even now, though you retain your strength. *Here today, gone tomorrow,* the saying goes. Yet the King has things for us that we cannot see now but will celebrate later. We both will see him in good time, as we will then see ourselves, and not in only rough outline, but face to face. Then we will know one another even better. We *know only a portion of the truth*, but when the King arrives, he will show us everything.

So don't let my letter discourage you. Instead, take it with a grain of salt but one that makes life's every meal better. Take it as an invitation to dine with the King, or maybe to play in a rocking great band for him, *raising the roof* for him. Can anything be better? What a great way forward that would be, a way that seems new but is instead so old that as to be lost to most of us. It is so much about whom we imitate, isn't it, especially when we think we imitate no one? See, you and I can talk frankly now, leaving behind the polite talk for mature talk. Why should we imitate anyone other than him, when he is so far greater? The images we create hold an unhealthy power to capture us against our better desires to pursue his image. Yet you and I are putting behind ordinary ways to find extraordinary ways that only he can show us.

Please know that I want nothing for you less than your best. I want the same because I know it will last for both of us. We share a Father whose *richly embroidered coat* we both wear because he so favors us with his a *marvelous freedom of which we never would have dreamed*. Whether we are sick or well, prosperous or poor, we still wear that rich coat that distinguishes us from our circumstance. Others do not see gray, cold eyes in us but a light in our eyes that gives them confidence. We have that light because of the King who pressed us into his service, although we were glad to go, weren't we? That service is what helps me love you and watch with joy your own service for him. Because remember, his service is not hard but the lightest thing we could bear.

It may seem odd to us that the King wants to spend time with us, until we remember that he made us who we are. The danger of your own adventures reminds me that he made room in his creation for challenges, indeed battlefields. His wish though is that he loses no one in the battle but that everyone *has a whole and lasting life* before returning to him, which is why he fought the battle for us, to bring us back to him. In a sense, all we need do is to dress appropriately, which is to say, to dress in the unique royal clothing that he makes for each of us. When we return following the battle of kings, we each bring him our own gifts that he asked of us. He *shaped us first inside then out*, indeed in the womb of the mother whom we shared *before we saw the light of day*. We hope to carry our gifts back to him triumphantly, before the end of our days he so exquisitely numbers unknown to us.

Here, though, is the point of my letter, friend. How we should know this rich way back to him without making some study of it? Why should we even seek it unless we know how great the adventure is and how rich the reward for completing it? In fact, the way to him requires that we rely on his power, *not a brute strength but a glorious inner strength*. How should we receive that strength without knowing its source in him? The simple truth is that we cannot find the path or reach that reward without him. It would be like trying to wash ourselves without water, when he is the one who would *pour pure water over us and scrub us clean*. We need him as that agent.

You are so accomplished, far more so than me, though a few people think I too have accomplished a few things. You and I have fitted ourselves for every activity of our own. We should fit ourselves equally for our ultimate journey. Isn't paradise worth it? We should *take a good look at the way we are living* using something than our own measure, instead using his better measure. School taught us reason. We then trained many more years to acquire the skills for our vocations. We spared little in those pursuits, whether finances, friendships, or indeed even the King's ransom. We fit ourselves at much expense for our own hobbies and recreations. We pursue fancies as short-lived as the morning fog and as sadly incapable of winning for us the King's reward.

Understand, dear brother, that he has no wish to change your service or mine, or to change those with whom we would share our time and blessings. We may *stay where we were when* the King called us. Instead, our hearts gradually change as we begin living his fullness and breathing his purpose. Yet again, how do we gain his fullness without giving him the time of day? If only we did so, then he would satisfy and reward us.

So many know so little of him. The worldly are sophisticated only in the things of the world. They are fools in the King's eyes, not even having a working knowledge of who he is, no less real insight into his character. They are *embarrassed by their handmade gods*, dead things next to the King's living wisdom that shapes the world. They know nothing of spiritual principles, no less the King's spiritual text. Instead, they are *lovers of emptiness, of nothing, so out of touch with reality, so far gone.* They devour contemporary writings out of spiritual hunger that those writings cannot satisfy because spiritual innocents write them. Their writings are *useless for either good or evil.* Not to overstate things, my friend.

The literate know of the King's text, even if they do not know the King whom his text describes or know that his text also describes them in their own attributes and condition. They just have the *bad habit of not listening* to what is good for them. For what trivia do they give away our treasure? They get themselves *worked up over nothing.* By losing the King's gift, they not only lose their mooring but lose the fullness of life that comes from relationship with the divine author. No one feeds them. Some try, but none can, for only the King satisfies.

Why do so many of the most intellectual and educated among us not know the nature and organization, if not the power and authority, of the King's unparalleled text? His text conveys his attributes so clearly that he is constantly *showing up in the good things we do* so that others see the King in us as we pursue that great reward that he achieved for us. We *study how he did it.* They only guess, and guess wrongly, at his attributes—a method they would never follow in anything else important, indeed even those things of far less consequence. They believe themselves to be better designers and illustrators of their own lives, when they are only his illustration. Arrogant fools they are, *having no idea who the King is, lured away from him by the latest speculations,* and so being incapable even of distinguishing good from evil. They write their own stories rather than live as they do within his story.

They should see instead that step by misguided step they arrive lost at unintended destinations, by daily dissipation and distraction. They abandon him for the mundane, the *sharp edge of their expectation dulled by things like shopping.* They neglect him because they do not read and study the right things about him. *Know-it-alls, they know everything but* the King's text. They fill day after day with idleness rather than get to know him. They think he lives only in a church when he lives instead inside us and we live in him. We need to *lay out the truth to them, plain and simple.* He knows where they are headed, and *what he says goes.* They think his words are all washed up, when instead what he says gives us the energy to move forward.

Look, I don't mean to be hard on anyone, good friend. Let's just blame the current culture that many otherwise-smart folks today just never got introduced to the King's text. They just never started reading it, rejecting it before it ever had a chance with them. They recognize some phrases such as that the King would have them luxuriate in the greenest pastures and would provide their daily bread. Yet they cannot locate or place those obvious jewels within the other rich fields of his incomparable text. They use his text's phrases without even knowing that they came from him and when those phrases standing alone lose their power and purpose. Eloquence means nothing. *No one gets by on muscle alone,* nor on charm or wit. We all need substance.

Maybe the information age is to blame. They soak up new information endlessly. Their reading fits their consumptive lifestyles. They discard what they read just like they throw away containers, cameras, and clothing. Streams of reading material pass before their eyes before floating forever out of their consciousness. While a few classics used to inform them, indeed the King's text was once their great guide, now they do a *lot of frantic running around, trying to figure out what's going on*—feeling almost a physical illness while searching among literally books-a-million. Then they call that aimlessness a gain of knowledge. They need a guide, dear brother, a *Spirit of Truth to take us by the hand* to diagnose like an anthropologist or sociologist their strangely linear illness.

Maybe we still think that we are pioneers who must discover and settle new lands, now only along imaginary frontiers of the mind. Grade school to graduate school, we absorb fresh information repeatedly, just long enough to repeat that on examination. Each term brings us new texts, always, new texts. Yet *being up-to-date with the times* is not to be wise. Wisdom comes instead from deep understanding of the King's text. Nonetheless, our endlessly linear reading makes quaint the idea that we could dwell instead in any single text, even one so long, complex, and unfathomably rich as the King's text. Tell someone you read a book twice, memorizing some of its passages, and they will look at you as if you were crazy. While they stand by the information stream, they never look up-river to the source.

This searching for new meaning is nothing really new. The King's text says that the ancients also pursued the latest *catchy opinions to tickle their fancy.* Even after the King introduced himself to them, showed himself as the master, they still *subjected themselves again to paper tigers.* You, though, hold on to sensibility, Memphis. Knowledge increases, but love and wisdom do not increase. For wisdom and love, we must know knowledge's author, the King who is love. Education may require reading widely. We would then be better if, once educated, we pursued our prime text consistently and deeply to develop our minds and lives. Instead, they continue reading and by doing so gradually embrace *an alien message, a no-message, a lie* about the King. They search without knowing him for whom they look, without knowing that they are even looking, following reading habits that they do not even recognize as a choice and peculiar.

We, though, turn toward the King's story, not only knowing its value but also knowing that we have a part in it. We read and relish the essential. By doing so, we participate with the King rather than watch from the sidelines where we would win only our own destruction. By working the King's words into our own words, the King's thoughts into our own thoughts, we build solid footing, *fixed to the rock,* steadied by him, made stable where we were once insecure. We change, renew, and grow, sometimes stepping, other times leaping closer to our full capacity for life, love, and reason.

I hear you and agree, dear Memphis, that many reject the King out of dislike for the traditions and attitudes of those whom they mistakenly believe to be his kingdom's prime inhabitants. They should not let those impostors fool them. While the King says that they *must get along with each other*, instead those impostors divide his house. They argue and gossip. They turn the gift of his company into rules and doctrine, and then they turn that doctrine into controversy. Do not let them distract you, dear brother. Do we turn our eyes from a painted masterpiece because its curators dispute its ownership? Do we refuse to listen to a classic song because of competing claims to its copyright? The same can happen to anything and anybody, but we must not allow arguments about him to dissuade us from him.

Many of those who dwell in his house have also lost contact with the King's text. By doing so, they have lost sight of the King, having a *reputation for vigor but stone dead.* His house can be a comforting place. Some favor that comfort over proximity to the King. While he affords us his comfort as we need it, he purpose is not our ease. He wants something more meaningful from us and for us, which is to grasp his message again and by doing so share in his life and story. We are desperate without it. Our challenge, though, is practical, not philosophical or doctrinal, to weave his text into our lives that we become a part of his movement through history. Good works distract even devout readers. We all face that challenge. Relationship takes commitment. Relationship takes work. The best remedy is to remember the *gift we once had in our hands* and let that memory and the reading it inspires turn our inner dialogue back to him.

Have I overstated the case, Memphis, that to lose touch with the King's text is to lose one's life? I mean what I say that we stake our lives on this question. We *die once, then face the consequences.* We must *know how to encourage tired people,* which is to let the King wake them up. To grow tired and sleep is death, when to pursue the King's word is life. *Good life begins in the fear* of the King, meaning that we must attend first to him. We have a fortune in him. What would it have been like to live before his time, under a precious collection of laws but only his foreshadowing — to have the question but not the answer, the taste but not the teaching? He came *not to demolish but to complete, to pull it all together in a vast panorama.* The moment of his coming for us would have been to *walk in darkness and to see a great light.* Of this event we should read — and celebrate.

Be sure, though, that I am not writing about empty religious talk. The King hates *religious sales talk* that draws people away from him. That talk is not the source of life. That talk has no power over the things that destroy people, things like addictions. Everyone knows how powerful those destructive things are. While not all of us share the same temptations to destruction, all of us have some. We can identify with those whom addictions destroy. We know that somewhere in our lives, we need that special power to resist and so move forward past the things that attract and destroy us.

The King gives us that special power, *breathing life on these slain bodies* in which we live. His story does not simply warn us about these things. His story draws us out of ourselves, which is critical because we are our own sources of temptation. From day one, we have thought of none more than we think of our own selves, making gods of our comforts, dreams, and anxieties. Dying from addiction or disease is terribly hard, but one could at least see one's demise coming, while still surrounded by love. To die alone indulged wholly within one's self must be perfect misery. Yes, friend, the King's story means life when it frees us from the greatest of all obstacles, that of ourselves.

I am not writing solely of spiritual mysteries, my good friend. Like you, I am a pragmatist, practical in all things, probably even too much a bottom-liner. Yet that practicality is precisely the point. The King speaks with perfect reason, indeed reason much clearer than our own. He keeps us on the path of reasonableness when our own thinking would lead us far from it. His text gives us an embarkation point, a touchstone for every decision. Families, groups, or organizations in which no one reads his text have no such guide star, no starting or ending point around which to pattern behavior. They have no basis from which to respond reliably to crises. They are *hot one day, cold the next, two-faced.* Everything is relative. They lurch from crisis to crisis, testifying to one another about their defeats and fearful of what bad thing will happen next.

Worse yet, they blame God for their troubles while taking credit for their victories. That thinking is the opposite of the King's thought. He says himself that "*the way I think is beyond the way you think.*" Blaming the King for miseries while believing blessings earned is deadly because it is neither being *honest with him or about him.* It only discourages others from getting to know him through his text. We who know the King's text know better. Those who believe themselves cursed by God have mistaken their friend and ally for their enemy, when their friend has full power over that enemy. They have turned friendly fire on the only one who could help them.

One thing we should admit, good friend: reading the King's text takes some discipline. It can take intensity, in which we would not want to *drag our feet*. Yet we ought not to blame the King's text for being distant or impenetrable. Remember, its words and events are so accessible as to have made their way into our everyday language when we don't even know it, turning the King's words into common idioms. That accessibility is the way he wanted it. We just have to see his message behind the idioms. We need only to grasp our inheritance. Would mom and dad leave our inheritance to a stranger? Inheritance depends on relationship. Relationship depends on diligent and patient attention. We should want to know the King *personally, to experience his resurrection power.*

To anyone who complains about the difficulty of reading the King's text, looking for our sympathy, let us remind them gently of the King's love chapter. Its language is so plain that an eight-year-old child can understand it, even while it inspires poets. Introduce them to the King's story written by the one whom the King especially loved. Show them the King's prophet calling down fire on the King's enemies or another prophet pointing his fearful servant's gaze to God's rescuing legions. Open their eyes to the collection of proverbs, the tender book of the widow, or the emotion of psalms. Share with them the King's incomparable message from the mount. Point them to the King, for in him they will find rescue.

No one need be a scholar to read the King's text. We each receive our own insight. Education is no obstacle. We hear insightful applications of the King's text from uneducated persons held in jail cells, not just from pulpits. When we are low enough, stripped of our wealth and status, we too can catch the insight. The King speaks not through wind, fire, and earthquake but in *gentle and quiet whisper.* Our hearing depends on us, not on the speaker, who is always available and *keeps his commitments across generations.*

The rest of this letter, my dearest friend, is not a study of the King's text. I have no qualifications to offer one. We must each discover on our own or with the guide of others more knowledgeable. We have plenty of help that way. My purpose is instead to encourage both of us in reading the King's text more consistently, actually reading it rather than letting others with bad attitudes tell us what they think about it. Let us each open it at regular intervals to let the King's words pass directly into our consciousness. I mean here only to turn our attention to our reading practices and attitudes, not to the content of his message, which you should instead receive directly from him. I urge this course with the simple hope that *your love will flourish and that you will not only love much but love well.*

Imagine, Memphis. We prosper simply by allowing the King's word to reside within us. I remind you of this wonder because I love you, though my love is only the palest imitation of the King's incomparably rich love. My love is vain and fleeting. His love is divine. My love encourages you momentarily. His love transforms you forever. I give you a little out of what I have, though I wish to give you more. He gives you everything he has and weeps that you would accept more. Read his story with me, Memphis. Read of his love. *Everything I once thought I had going for me is insignificant* next to his love. Let us rediscover together the King's great text and so let rise between us his promised gift of life. Let him lead us out of Egypt. *God rides on a fast-moving cloud, moving in on Egypt! The god-idols of Egypt shudder and shake, paralyzed by panic.*

He had yearned for this moment as long as he could remember. Yet now that the moment was here, he discovered to his surprise that something was not yet evident to him. He had hoped for that one thing, beyond his own merciful admission into this paradise. He felt no sorrow or confusion over not knowing the answer. This place would admit no such disquiet. All was fulfillment. He was overjoyed to be in the King's paradise at last, where he was constantly and supernaturally aware of the King's glorious presence. Nothing whatsoever could possibly diminish the utter satisfaction of such continual nearness.

Still, he did not yet know whether he would meet here his beloved brother. He had thought that he would instantly know of all the kingdom's fellow residents. He had expected an instant answer to his brother's salvation but did not have one. In retrospect, like so many other things, he had been mistaken. God, not paradise's residents, was omniscient. Indeed, why should he know immediately of his brother's admission? The King would reveal the answer to him in perfect timing, of that he knew. Until then, he would revel in the glory of the King, adding to it with his whole heart as did all other residents each in their own measure.

The King's paradise held other surprises for him, beyond the surprise that he could not yet discern whether all those to whom he had been closest in his earthly life were also paradise's residents. Those surprises took two forms. One was that the King's word that this new resident had so treasured in his earthly life described the King's paradise more concretely than the new resident had imagined. He had mistaken many of the word's references to be symbolic rather than literal. He had read of fruit, trees, jewels, and rivers, expecting something like those things but yet somehow different. Instead, he found and delighted that fruit was fruit, trees were trees, and rivers were rivers. Paradise had a reality to it that was more real than the earthly was real. In retrospect, he should have known that the earthly things were the representations and that the kingdom's things would be real.

The other surprise was how simply the King's paradise resolved what in the earthly life were vexingly complex issues. Here, picking fruit did not damage or diminish the trees. Every tree bore just as much fruit as it should to satisfy at all times all residents. No one picked more fruit than needful. No picked fruit wasted. He ate fruit to enjoy it, not to satisfy hunger, of which the land admitted none. Likewise, great rivers ran impressively but always within their course, without flooding or even impeding travelers. One could cross a great river enjoying its playful wetness but emerge from the river safe and dry, all without taxing effort. No person, condition, event, or action threatened, diminished, or damaged anything.

Was his brother enjoying the realm? He simply did not know the answer. Nor did he have any sense when he would learn the answer. Until then, he rested assured that the King would reveal it to him in just the manner that would most glorify the King while preserving the perfection of this most extraordinary kingdom. He could not imagine the kingdom lessened by the absence of his beloved brother, even though he could also not imagine a perfect kingdom from which his brother would be absent. He would simply glorify the King with his whole heart until the King revealed the answer to him.

2

Who

He tucked the blade of grass that had fallen into his lap from the tall stands along the riverbank into his place near the beginning of his brother's long letter. He then folded the letter back into the brown paper, tying the string again securely around it. How like his brother, he thought, to leave him to his adventures while sharing his own thoughts only in text that he could either take or leave as his adventures permitted him. He would read more later. Right now, he must turn his attention again to navigating the river town at which the boat had just arrived.

He had much to accomplish in the next few hours before sundown. He would be purchasing supplies in town for the desert journey to the ancient civilization's greatest ruins. He would embark on camel in the desert chill well before sunrise, to make camp in oasis shade by the rising heat of mid-morning. He would read more of his brother's letter later, as he camped through the mid-day heat before resuming the journey in the late evening. He decided, though, to move the letter from his trunk to his pack, keeping it nearer him. He recalled again with another pang of regret that his brother had not looked well at his departure, when he had handed him the letter. If the conductor had not called just then, he was sure that he would have asked after his brother's health and the welfare of his family.

He felt the jerk of the boat against the dock. Rising, he placed the brown-paper-wrapped letter in his pack with his notes and maps, and slung the pack across one shoulder. The boat rocked slightly as he made his way forward to the gangplank. He could already see the suppliers pushing forward, preparing to make their pitches. He noticed one supplier standing a way back rather than pushing forward with the others. They caught one another's eyes, nodding briefly at one another. The supplier turned briskly and walked off into town. He pointed to the receding supplier while giving a quick order to the boatman. He then descended the gangplank to push his way through the crowd of suppliers and follow the lone supplier into town. The boatman smiled admiringly. This traveler knew the ways of the world.

This letter is about you and me, Memphis—not about those who have no vision, seek no insight, or do not read, not about our neighbors, but about you and me. You and I must attend to reading, reading the right thing, meaning reading the King's text. Time is short. We must not let the opportunity slip away to *acquire a thorough understanding of the ways in which* the King works. Only that way do we know how we best work. The King's text is for us, not for others. We have the need as much as do others. We should not let our blind spot, which keeps us from seeing ourselves, keep us from seeing our own need. We see others clearly but cannot see ourselves. The King's text helps us overcome that tendency and instead look directly at ourselves, to *set ourselves apart* to *live the way* the King helps us.

You know that my service for the King has included visiting jail inmates, where you would think many need the King. The King himself says, *I was in prison and you came to me*. The first thing that a man in jail will tell you is that he is not a common criminal—not like others around him in jail. He may say that he was doing pretty well but just slipped up. Few if any admit to having poorly informed themselves. You do not hear "I am messed up" but rather "I messed up." The convicted treat their wrongs as if apart from themselves, not a product of their own thinking, as if their right hand knew nothing of what their left hand had done.

Yet we act consistent with our thinking. Thought precedes willful action. We think and then act, making critical the source of our thinking, which determines the quality of our acts. When our thoughts are callous, then so are our actions. When our thoughts are prideful and arrogant, then so are our actions. We should *give freely and spontaneously, without stingy hearts*. But do we do so? We incline to the opposite, *having this bent toward evil from an early age*. Our thoughts draw us toward selfish things, requiring that we resist that nature. We need something to help us put off *everything connected with that way of death*. New circumstance forces us to draw on old thought, making the quality of that thought continuously important. We are what we think.

The first thing we tell ourselves is that we are not like those who are in jail, that we have nothing in common with the prisoner. What one finds instead is that those in jail have nothing very peculiar about them. *There is no difference between us and them.* Of this truth I am confident, despite what geneticist might try telling us. Jail inmates do not have some rare crime gene. We are masters of our own genetics, at least on that moral level at which we make decisions of right and wrong. We possess power over our actions. The thoughts and actions that get prisoners in jail are like the thoughts and actions of the rest of us. They magnify those thoughts here and there, but they are not distinct thoughts. We all share those thoughts and inclinations, which are familiar to all of us.

Our consciences convict us. We harbor the same inclinations as any other. We have compiled a *long and sorry record, proving ourselves incapable.* At age two, none of us was crying out for justice for our fellow. We were not much better at age 12 or 20. We all share that ingrained selfishness. As much as I love you, my brother, we are alike when it comes to natural inclinations. Nor are those inclinations because of mistake. Rather, our thinking drives our inclinations and desires, when we have little guide for regulating our thinking. Conscience tempers our inclinations only ineffectively. We know the *futility of devising some system for getting by on our own efforts.* Following rules is not enough and never has been, or we would have complied by now. The King's text bringing the King's influence is effective.

The challenge is that we recognize our need for it. The moment we think that we are good enough not to attend to our daily reading practices, we judge ourselves more in control and better than we are. Adam and Eve made that error of ignoring God's command. *The tree looked like good eating,* and so they ate. We think that we can decide questions for ourselves, without consulting standards, even the King's standards. We rely on our own standards rather than acknowledging and relying on timeless external standards. God does not tell us what to wear each morning. Yet we should seek guidance in meaningful actions— and then listen. We listen when we read the King's text to discern his standards. We listen when we daily read that text to draw on its consistent message. We do *best when we fill our minds and meditate on things true, authentic, and compelling.* To draw on the

King's power to fulfill our purpose, we must read how others respond to his story and receive the consequences. His text reveals not only himself but us as we respond to him. The King's text teaches what is essential to an authentic and sound life.

Folks today are little different from the people the King's text describes. Individual character and social relations are today as they were in antiquity. The King's text shows the ancient characters to be perfectly modern in their attributes and tendencies. We are no less often despairing, overreaching, confused, rejected, or covetous. The ancients' experiences are remarkably modern. Are we any less often travelers, friends, strangers, leaders, or followers, than were the characters about whom we read in the King's text? Their experience of the King and his ancient paths are as relevant to us today as in their day, indeed more so because they have withstood the test of time. I want those old lessons, my friend. We should *ask for directions to the old road, the tried-and-true road* that we find in the King's text.

Ancient paths remain sound because the King *doesn't change — yesterday, today, tomorrow, he's always totally himself.* His attributes do not change with the ages or seasons. Ancient characters may have ridden donkeys down dirt paths rather than wheeled vehicles down superhighways. Machines do not change human character. The context carries no greater import than the message. We flee from pursuers figuratively, as the ancients fled literal pursuers. We face mountains figuratively, as the ancients faced literal mountains. We take stands figuratively, as the ancients took literal stands against enemies. The conditions that challenge us do not change, meaning that the responses should not change. The King certainly does not change. He *can't break his word, and because his word cannot change, his promise is likewise unchangeable.*

For example, can't we learn from the way in which the King's text describes the experience of the ancient prophet Elijah, running from his enemies? Elijah's flight can look a lot like our own purposeless action. God promptly called Elijah back to his mission, just as the King calls us to our luminous purpose. With Elijah, we are *sons of light and daughters of day.* We should listen to the King turning us back from our flight, leading us away from despair. Whom should we fear? From whom do we hide? What power does anyone have over us, when we follow the King? The King urges us to *go back the way we came.* Often, the place from which we run is our place. That place may be a mess. Like Elijah, we may have had victory there or faced threats there. Yet times may demand that we stay in that place to face the next challenge rather than run to places we do not belong. The King says, *I've refined you, but not without fire.* His plan for us does not include hiding. When we read deeply enough of the King's text, we see ourselves in the story of Elijah. Others refuse his refining fire. They withdraw from challenges, rejecting their purpose, not knowing Elijah's experience.

We also know the experiences of Deborah, Hannah, Ruth, Esther, David, Mephibosheth, and so many others whom the King's text features. Their lives and experiences enrich our own. We learn from them and the consequences of their thinking, decisions, and actions. We are these figures, Memphis. They and we together are "who" of the King's text. We must see ourselves in their lives if we are to have the full life that the King desires for us. We must allow their experiences, attitudes, and actions to instruct us. *I could go on and on, but I've run out of time. There are so many more—Gideon, Barak, Samson... .* All are there for our instruction. Whether heroes or fools, the figures teach us. We learn from Jeremiah's weeping, Isaiah's inspiration, and David's devotion.

Indeed, we have more to learn from others' errors than their successes. Consider Israel's first king, Saul, chosen not for wisdom but for looks, when Israel *wanted nothing to do with God but wanted a king.* The King's text first introduces us to Saul as he searches fruitlessly for his father's wandering donkeys, which is hardly a leader's task. Saul even asks the advice of his servant and some girls they encounter as they search, again hardly indication of a leader's discernment. When the great prophet Samuel greets Saul, Saul is so lacking in discernment that he asks Samuel if he has seen Samuel. *"I'm the seer,"* Samuel had to say. Many even knew that Saul had no capacity to lead, saying at his anointing, *"Don't make me laugh!"* Yet people today follow their own image of a leader, even those lacking discernment like Saul. They accept the short-lived comfort of letting someone who looks like a leader make decisions for them. They choose leadership not for its skill but for the image they have of leaders and of themselves.

We instead choose the true leader King, my friend. We accept leadership for its pursuit of the King and his character, looking for *humility, quiet strength, and discipline.* We learn from Saul's life, however bitter its course and ending. We, like Saul, must be sure that we are right for a job and it right for us. We, like Saul, must take the right action with the right motive. We must listen to the right counsel, make the right decisions, and implement those decisions fully and patiently, as the King's text instructs. Remember, we are the subjects of the King's text. We do not judge the text. It judges us. We should see ourselves and instruction for us in the lives of the King's figures. Whether those characters are flawed or gifted, they are for our instruction.

Yet the King's text holds much for us beyond mere lessons. We are spiritual in nature, animated and discerning in ways that other beings are not. We are not just body and mind, animal-like, but imbued with consciousness and, beyond consciousness, with conscience, with attitude, and thus with spirit. *The seed sown is natural; the seed grown is supernatural.* Coaches, psychologists, therapists, teachers, and trainers all know that spirit influences character, influences outcomes, influences lives and even generations. Those who reject everything spiritual, despite its evidence and power, sell their human birthright, like Isaac's wildman brother Esau, who, hungry, asked, *What good is a birthright if I'm dead?*

We do not sacrifice our spirituality to feed appetites that we cannot quench. Because we have the King, *bread on the table and shoes on the feet are enough* for us. While others sculpt and fragrance their bodies, we inform our minds and transform our spirits. We follow the King's plan knowing that our bodies and minds live by his Spirit. When we trust the King, we know that *his Spirit is in us — living and breathing God.* They kill themselves with stress, spirits of anxiety dulling their minds to purposeful and creative thinking. They live as if life had nothing more to it than satisfying desires, looking always for just the right mix of serenity and stimulation. Yet they fail to see their resulting malaise as a spiritual condition. Their minds so crave entertainment that they forget spiritual life and understanding. Body and mind mix with and bend to spirit, but they give no attention to the greater spiritual dimension.

Without the King's dimension, they consume themselves, mind living for body and body for mind, in a deadly circle with no outlet. Living for themselves rather than the King, they exchange the King's gift for self-help bestsellers. Just when the King's text would reveal them to themselves and make them each unique *in his image,* they instead read spiritless works encouraging them to discover, love, and rely on themselves. They destroy their freedom by doing *whatever they want to do.* Sensible persons following the King's text see their narcissism for what it is, life's end rather than its beginning. They accept everything they read. We *check out everything* against the King's text, accepting only what is good.

Following their writings, they look back to relive broken childhoods, while we read the King's text *beckoning us onward* to him. They critique their parents, while we read the King's text urging us to *honor our father and mother.* They negotiate with their spouses, while we read the King's text urging us to treat *marriage as a decision to serve the other.* They conceive of themselves as boilers needing to blow off steam at those who offend them, while we read the King's text to let *love make up for practically anything.* Their encounter groups practice rage therapy, like animals stripping one another of the vestiges of self-control and civility until they are *smeared with filth inside and out.* They turn relationships primal, when the King would heal and protect in relationships. Their therapeutic view of themselves tends to magnify woes and minimize blessings.

Today's idols are not stone and wood but false wisdom and reason. We properly remind ourselves and warn others that false wisdom is common. As the King's followers, we should *pass on his counsel* because the problem is unthinking acceptance of false alternatives. Those who accept secular counsel do not abandon all truth. Popular wisdom can reflect aspects of truth, particularly as it gives our problems contemporary context. Self-help writings do not supply the King's bedrock perspective. They do not help us distinguish truth from error. They do not help us distinguish what to save from what to reject. Error catches those who lack the foundation from which to judge it. By refusing to follow the King, he *banishes them to their chosen world of lies and illusions.* Without sensibility, they do not know what to save and reject. Popular wisdom does not teach them that sensibility. Only the King's text supplies it. When we eat fruit from his tree, he makes us *capable of knowing everything* that he knows about us.

The King's text tells us just how powerful his words are to shape our thoughts. They demolish mental and emotional traps into which our thinking falls, along the way *smashing warped philosophies.* They impeach our pretensions, *fitting every loose thought and emotion and impulse* into the King's shape for life. The King's text contains truths that no adversary can contradict. Everything teaches us with a *steady, constant calling and warm, personal counsel,* until it characterizes us. The King's text provides the rock on which we moor our attitude, mood, and consciousness. Why should we patch together some other life's guide when the King's text offers us the richest possible conception of our lives? I would have nothing less for you, my dearest brother, than to be filled with the King himself, *your body a sacred place* for the King's Spirit exactly as he made it.

The way in which we think of ourselves defines and confines our capacity. The King's true identity for us offers us such greater capacity than popular self-conceptions offer. To be a sacred place within which the King's Spirit dwells is a rich understanding. *Immense in mercy and with an incredible love, he embraced us.* We have only to accept his embrace, acknowledge our true identity, to begin to fulfill our capacity. You have always been a more astute observer, quicker of intellect and wit, than me, my dear brother. I am so encouraged that you too see how rich our inner sanctuary is, from which we radiate the Spirit's fullness. The King's text describes his temple as filled with sacred artifacts covered in gold. We see the possibility, indeed the truth, that *everything is clean to the clean-minded*, that we can be such a sanctuary. The King's text burns away the dross of our purposeless activity, refining out of it the gold of his presence. We need only endure and persevere through that refinement, to *strip down, start running, and never quit,* to radiate the fullness and glory of his Spirit. The more we accept his refining work, yielding to his image for us, the quicker his work will occur in us.

I know that you have gold at your core, my dear brother. Our role is to build our inner sanctuary so that the King will bring more. David's son Solomon built the King a physical temple like none ever seen, into which he placed sacred articles. *So let's get moving and build our sacred house.* We have the King's text, the King's Spirit, the King's treasures, to store. We need not worry that our minds and spirits have ossified. The King's message is like fire, like a *sledgehammer busting rock.* The King's text helps us build a sanctuary within us for his love, courage, and compassion. We let nothing else into our inner sanctuary, not the wound of friend or enemy, nor anxiety, fear, or pride. Only the King's Spirit enters, carried within by his word, producing his *famous and righteous ways*.

Outside of our inner sanctuary we have an altar to give back to the King. We return to him our service, in the quiet work we do for him and his others. In that sacrifice we receive our own sustenance because *those who work in the temple live off the proceeds of the temple.* We live not to consume for our own pleasure but to share in his pleasure, in communing circle. Beyond our altars, we have outer courts where we deal with the world, not in the posture with which we approach the King, so that we don't *trivialize our holy work* in our inner sanctuaries. The world wars against our spirits, and so we hold the world at bay, allowing only the King to enter our inner sanctuary. *Only the high priest enters.* We meet the world in our outer courts beyond the walls of our inner sanctuary. The world gives us that which we sacrifice on our altars back to him, through ministry and mission for the King's glory.

Brother, I see through your abundant intellectual and physical gifts that inner sanctuary to which you aspire. Out of our inner sanctuaries then flow rivers of living water, *water pouring out from the temple,* wide and deep, *water that no one could walk through.* The King's waters flow out from us to nourish others even as he nourishes us, *gushing fountains of endless life.*

The King's identity for us does not turn us inward but directs his power out from us to heal others in his most beneficent Spirit. The King gives us wondrous self-images. In his magnificent parables, we are the soil and seed, branches on his vine, the fruit-bearing tree. Our hope is the tiny seed flowering into a great tree sheltering his most delicate of creations. We are the wildflower, reed, grass, and sparrow. The King's text gives us so many rich ways to think of ourselves, each rich because from him. We can't lose because *alive, we are the King's messenger, dead his bounty.*

Yet, my friend, the King's text has one other person at its center beyond us, and that person is the glorious King himself. He must be at the center of his text because *everything got started in him and finds its purpose in him.* The main character of the King's text is not Abraham, nor Moses, nor David, but the King himself. Much of the King's text involves ordinary people like Jacob, Isaac, and Peter, though in extraordinary encounters. The King nonetheless suffuses his text, his absence as significant to those figures as his presence. The same is true today. The King's continues his influence. History marches to his tune. His text revealed his character not to document his impact on those figures but to proclaim his availability to all of us for ages. As evidence, we have only to look down through history at the leaders who followed him, to *look at the way they lived and let their faithfulness instruct us.* The King's text is both history and beyond history, his continuing story.

Contemporary philosophers do not accurately describe the King's qualities, although we find his influence everywhere, even in their writings. When he revealed himself and his purpose, he created a foundation for all subsequent thought, even when, and especially when, that thought tries to contradict him. When a modern writer says that the King is dead, that writer is only lending the King due honor as the one with whom all must first deal. We know from the King's text that he is not the king of *dead men but of the living* — a living King to whom all are alive. We need only acknowledge his leadership in order to live, God *doing in us what he did in raising* the King. If they see the King's traces in contemporary writings, then they should read the King's text to see the full King, *from the waist up like burnished bronze and from the waist down like a blazing fire.*

Friend, see the jet's power in the jet itself rather than in the traces of its icicle trailing. Let not one word of how modern authors describe the King supplant how he revealed himself to us. We are *not here to demolish but to complete* his story. A critic's review captures little of the actual performance while running significant risk of misrepresenting it. We do not accept descriptions of the King that depart from the text through which he revealed himself to us. You are so much wiser than to accept any substitute. No mind of any age could ever be a truer reporter of his glorious character of rationality, wisdom, discretion, sensitivity, justice, mercy, and compassion. He is *the King, the only King there is.* His text gives us the one true revelation of him. When we read the King's text, we see his attributes as his own words describe him. *We warn people not to add to his message.*

Is the King merciful, and if so, then when? Is he just, and if so, then for what causes? Does he love us, and if so, then when we have what heart and take what action with what motivation? Is he a King who chooses, and if so, then what moves him to exercise that discretion? The answers to these questions are critically important to us and those around us because they dictate our destinies. We must discern those answers from reliable source, for we cannot trust our own judgment. The *heart is hopelessly dark and deceitful, a puzzle that no one can figure out.* The King knows our hearts, judging us as we are and guiding us as he knows we need. He condemns our pride and self-idolatry. He likes us contrite, as we ought to be. We need not guess at his desires for us, consult a medium, or read tea leaves. We need only read his text, from which our hearts draw clear answers. The King writes our life as a *letter that anyone can read.*

The King reveals his attributes gradually throughout his text, which is good because we could not comprehend him at once. His glory would be frightening on frank display, annihilating us. The King shields his glory. He places us in the *cleft of the rock,* covering us with his hand and showing us only his back once he passes by. Frank presentation would not fit his glory. The King's text would do disservice cataloguing his attributes, which must instead appear within the panorama from creation to apocalypse. The text unfolds the King's character within a history that makes it meaningful to us, his *mystery kept secret for so long but now an open book.* We see him first as creator, then provider, judge, and nation-founder. We see him then incarnate, so tender in heart and so healing in presence as to be love himself. We see him then as the descending Spirit alighting followers with the Spirit's flames. His unfolding attributes set in the march of world history fit his glory, which he then lends to us, *commissioning us as his judges.*

So great is our King that no single name can describe him. His names change throughout his text. He is God and then the Lord and Lord God, with all feudal implications that we remain *reverently responsive to what he says.* Lord in the Hebrew language he spoke it sounds like I AM, which he also calls himself in frightening encounter with Moses. He is indeed the mysterious whole of being. We also see him as the Fear, one for whom we hold that respectful kind of fear one has for a justly stern father. Then he is the Presence, the omniscient one who knows our thoughts and motives. Then he is the Judge bringing consequences commensurate with the quality of our actions. Then he is the Watcher of Men, the Rock, the Redeemer, my Banner, Emmanuel, the Son of Man, Jealous, the Holy One, the Name, Christ, Messiah, the Savior. The King's *life is a great mystery, far exceeding our understanding* but revealed in part in his names.

The King's attributes matter. I do not write here of metaphysics. I only write as your friend, of things of practical significance. The King's attributes save us from an otherwise meaningless condition. When our *minds are set on him,* he steadies and completes us. His character, not our work, nor chance or fortuity, carries us from situation to situation, indeed when we walk his way, from glory to glory, *our lives gradually becoming brighter and more beautiful* as he transfigures us. He is with us, and when he is with us, there are *more on our side than on their side.* The world's order is his order. Our own attributes, yes, yours and mine, Memphis, draw us into what we daily face, but the King's attributes bring us out. We have chosen him, my brother. We do not make an idol of chance, attributing events to luck or fortune. We acknowledge the King's hand in all things, good as his blessing and challenge as the refining of our faith in him. *Apart from faith,* we cannot please the King. He rewards our devotion to him.

Let me encourage you, my friend. My writing should fall lightly, not heavily, on your strong shoulders. When we rely on his attributes, the consequences can be quick and remarkable. A god of luck keeps them living from moment to moment, random lives without soul. We reject chance and instead see the King's hand at work everywhere. We immediately live a new life of purpose, even as *don't try to figure out everything on our own.* We trust the King, not even worrying about what to say or do. We do not plot and plan, running from person to person trying to say all the right things. We *don't worry about what we'll say or how we'll say it,* knowing the King will supply the words. We just rely on his attributes, his strength, compassion, protection, and provision, and simply trust him. When the King rescues, we accept it quickly and thankfully, fitting our trust in him. When he sends us doctors, we accept their healing, and his counselors, we listen to them. When he gives us peace in trouble, we rejoice in it. Under his care, the *wolf romps with the lamb.* Under his care, our lives take on his power and order. Reading his text is not about Abraham and Joseph but about our relationship to the magnificent King.

When we read of the King, one other person joins us: the one next to us, who may be our spouse, child, coworker, or neighbor. We learn that three exist in every relationship, just as the King is within the *Father, Son, and Holy Spirit.* When you and I come together, my brother, the King joins us. He shows us how to relate not only to ourselves but also to others. He urges us to *go all out in our love for our wives,* as he has gone all out in his love for us. These *things he wants us to teach.* That a husband would sacrifice for a wife contradicts today's thinking. Writers today, without the King, urge us to marry those who ask nothing of us, whom we need offer nothing, and to whom we need never apologize. Writers today, without the King, place the self at the center of every relationship, even marriage, expecting the other to accommodate, sacrifice, and serve. Imagine the marriages that such instruction is hurting.

The King instructs a husband's sacrifice for a specific purpose, that the wife may be blameless, radiant. No wife, indeed no one other than the King, could be without blame. We are all blameworthy. Yet the husband's role remains to conceive of and treat his wife as if she were blameless, just as the King's love makes us blameless. He *settled on us as the focus of his love, to be made whole and holy.* Others would tell a husband not to embarrass or wound his wife and instead to do that which will nurture her. The King says more, that the husband's purpose is to make his wife radiant. The King gives the true basis for marriage, with responsibility on the husband not to choose or shape a wife to the husband's standard but instead for the husband to follow the King's standard for the purpose that most benefits both husband and wife.

The King's instruction on how to relate to one another differs from the world's instruction. The *world doesn't know the first thing about living.* The world encourages parents to allow children to make their own decisions. Times change, the world says, and relationships must change with them. Parents are not wise and mature counselors but rather more like indulgent friends of their children. Parents allow their children to do things that they never would have done, biting their tongues not because they do not care but because the world teaches them to do so. *Don't fall for any line like that one.* The world asserts that each generation must discover new rules rather than learn from an elder generation, while the King says the opposite. *Discipline your children while you still have the chance.* Children obey when fathers bring their children up knowing the King, who says to *children to do what your parents tell you,* while cautioning parents not to exasperate their children. Our children hear us talk of the King's words until we *get them inside our children.*

You know me, my dear brother. I will speak to the child in love, but I will speak. We must be active watchmen, not sleeping. The King says *I'll hold the watchman responsible.* Our children live in the sleeping city, and so, watchman friend, speak with me. Give your wise counsel to my child and your own children. We obey the King's instruction for our children as much as we obey it for ourselves. Whenever you see my child, speak truth to her. Let her know the King's truth about our behavior and condition. Let her know your discoveries in order that she need not suffer as we suffered apart from the King.

We fear that we might lose the child's friendship. Yet if the child rebels over instruction, then both relationship and child are already broken. *If you warn the wicked to change and they don't do it,* then you are no longer responsible. We should tell others what worked for us, which is that the King freed us, because we are a *case study of what he does.* We are not preaching to others when we explain what happened to us. We instead show the greatest humility. We show that our willingness to change to meet his expectations made all the difference for us. We teach only when we have first learned, and we teach only from what we have learned following the King's instruction. We *cultivate these things, immerse ourselves in them,* knowing that none could have a stronger foundation.

The King's difference holds even in the workplace. The world encourages workers to seek jobs where upward mobility is greatest, that they should work for their own advancement. They have *great ambitions for themselves, but nothing comes of it.* If employers do not pay adequately, then employees do not work. If employees work hard without the employer taking notice, then they quit working and *grouse angrily to the manager.* The worker is a fool who does not sell services to the highest bidder. Yet they are unhappy working. Work burdens. They find it *useless to rise early and work worried fingers to the bone.* Work does not satisfy, having lost its meaning. Work is all *bad business,* humiliating rather than enriching. The paycheck is its only reward, and even that is too small and quickly gone and forgotten.

The King sees our work differently. He knows we need meaning in work, *peaceful repose better than fistfuls of worried work.* He urges us to work for him, even when we work for others, to *work heartily as his servants* because our work serves the King. We listen to our employers with sincerity and respect just as we would listen to the King, *obeying our earthly masters but with an eye to obeying our real master* the King. Our relationship to our employer includes the King. Three parties, not two, share our work. The third party, the King, gives work its meaning. We obey an employer not primarily to win our employer's favor but to please the King and *get us good pay* from the King. We conceive of work differently, for whom we are working. We serve the King, not merely men. We *work from the heart for our real master.* We serve our employers to serve the King.

When we work to obey the King, then the King rewards us, even under an unappreciative employer. The beautiful Abigail worked to save the life of her surly and undeserving master. She was *intelligent and good-looking, her master surly and mean.* Her reward was promotion into service of King David. We find new purpose and reward in our work when we work for the King. Obedient work gradually changes us, even as our obedience changes our work. We find ourselves serving in new places and ways. The King favors us with new challenges, responsibilities, and promotions. His work suits us. The King requires the same from employers as he does from employees, which is that employers serve their employees wholeheartedly. He *makes no distinction between them.* Both work for the King. We simply get on with the work he gives us. Why should we serve any lesser one than the King who created and cherishes us? Even in our work, our minds are on him. We *look up to what is going on around* the King. Those around us will take notice. Our King relationship defines us in the best light for others.

The King teaches us how to relate not only to spouses, children, and employers but also to governments, tax collectors, jailers, friends, enemies, parents, sisters, and brothers. We embrace and follow his instruction, my dearest Memphis. We look to nowhere else for lessons on relationships. We let the King's instruction lift our relationships. The King's text transforms not just our lives and perspectives but our relationships. We need not judge and criticize others to improve our relationships. We need only have faith that the King will change us, that he is the *firm foundation under everything that makes life worth living.*

Our relationships reflect our condition and character. We depend on the King's text and Spirit in those relationships. The King's text teaches us his character. We learn of him, just as we learn about ourselves and others, by reading. We discover who we are, who the King is, and who those around us are and how to relate to them. Together, we are the subjects of the King's text, dear Memphis. The King's text holds for us invaluable identity and relationship lessons. We look for those lessons elsewhere at our peril. *Doom to those who go off to Egypt thinking that horses can help them.*

In the meantime, while he waited to discover whether he would meet his beloved brother, he would explore this divine realm. He had been doing so since the moment of his entry. As he strolled along gentle paths, his spirit seemed to soak in the invigorating air saturated with the Master's presence. The paths were indeed gentle. He labored not at all. Perhaps the paths were not so gentle and that instead he had an unusual vigor, for his walking took him through the most spectacular country of hills and valleys with mountains alongside. His earthly life had ended in physical weariness, even if with undaunted spirit. Here, all weariness was gone. He had more than regained the energy of youth. Walking the bold country was effortless, refreshing, even restoring.

Walking also seemed like the most natural activity for him to do. He was in no anxious rush. He did not really even sense that he had a destination to achieve. He had many places to explore and people to meet, principal among them the great King whose presence he felt at every moment. Yet every moment in this place had its own completeness. Anticipation, while still present, diminished nothing of each moment. Each step along the path, breath of fresh air, and new vista were fully satisfactory in themselves, unburdened of the next moment. Only in this realm blessed with the unmediated presence of its fabulous King could one fully live in each moment. The new resident moved forward along the paths with his motion yet timeless, each frame fully formed in perfection that he had not known but only anticipated in his earthly dominion.

The thought had already occurred to him that he must have a home in this realm. He knew that he would because the King's word had promised it. He knew, too, that the King would have prepared his home to suit him perfectly. Anticipation of discovering it enriched each step, even as again he had no sense of needing to find it. Rest of the kind that an earthly home provided did not seem necessary with the King's presence supporting him at each step, although he knew that he would find rest in his divine home nonetheless. In the meantime, he could stop for rest anywhere along the paths, if he felt that he needed it or should enjoy it.

The new resident was already noticing other inhabitants as he walked. None approached him directly, but all seemed aware and appreciative of his passing, just as he was aware and appreciative of each of them. Each person whom he noticed was a literal stranger. Yet he instantly felt familiarity toward each of them, to the point of outpouring love. He barely recognized the root of the feeling from his earthly life. The feeling was akin to that which he might have had for a childhood best friend or an adult whom he had deeply admired. Here in the King's realm, he had that full feeling for every inhabitant whom he encountered. It quickly became one of his greatest joys of the realm, each time lifting him to new height in his appreciation for the love and splendor of the Master who authored it. The Master loved each resident as he loved the new resident. The new resident realized that the Master's love must suffuse all thought of each toward one another who reside together in his realm.

Just then, as he first connected his profound feeling for each resident with the King's own love, the new resident realized that his path was taking him to his first meeting with the King. For just an instant, the thought startled him. Then, he realized that the kingdom would of course permit no delay in the King's introduction. The King had his great seat before the assembly but also inhabited all parts of his realm, each of which was within his reach in an instant. No resident had need of entreating his presence. He would appear exactly when and where each resident desired him to do so, for the Master and each resident shared complete desire for and fulfillment in one another.

These thoughts had no sooner formed in the new resident's mind than he sensed the King walking beside him. The new resident began to weep in joy, tears streaming down his face and his sides heaving, even as they continued to walk along the broadened path. He scarce could look at the King's face. When he did, he wept more for seeing that the King wept with him. At that instant, the new resident lost the last speck of himself, knowing fully that he had finally gained all. For a moment, he wanted to collapse on the path and walk no farther. Instead, he felt the King's hand at his elbow urging him on. The King and his new resident simply walked along the path side by side, weeping and gathering themselves together, only to weep and gather some more. Then, the King was gone, in the perfect instant. The new resident felt no loss or longing whatsoever. He knew that the King would return as soon as his newest resident was once again ready.

3

What

The horizon simmered in the noonday heat outside the tent. He was relieved at the desert journey's start, even though he always enjoyed his interactions with local suppliers. Haggling with suppliers created a rare human bond in his journeys — not that he was looking for it. He had always thought of his adventures as great solo escapes. Society was not his goal but his reason for escape. His intentional isolation made all the more enjoyable the rare acquaintances that he made along the way. Transportation with a little sustenance, the more local the better, were his only needs. Comfort and privilege he did not ask. Safety and security were of no concern. His few needs not only made the haggling easier but also gained instant respect from the suppliers.

In this instance, the local supplier had been particularly willing to meet his few needs at reasonable price. They had not really even exchanged words. A few hand gestures and movements of the chin had sufficed. The camels would leave halfway through the night for the ruins. He had motioned toward what looked like a feed shed off the back of the supplier's hut. The supplier had nodded. He had dozed there through the evening and early night until the guide had roused him, camels at the ready. The first leg to the oasis had then been uneventful, the camels' rhythmic pace almost entirely unbroken.

It was now too hot to doze, with midday heat radiating off the sides of the tent. His attention turned again to his brother's letter in the pack beneath his head. He opened the pack, removed the paper-wrapped letter, and untied its strings, again with a smile at his brother's so-typical means of communicating. Why write a letter — what he should more accurately call a book? What was it about books, he thought, or about any book, that his brother could hold so important? He smiled again, this time at the answer that he already knew. While his adventures were physical, others adventured in the metaphysical. He knew the close connection between the two realms, indeed suspected at times that the two might be one. He also knew and respected his brother's metaphysical adventures.

Although the oasis was dead quiet in the midday still, without a hint of any breeze, the air outside the tent now seemed to buzz with heat. The heat did not bother him physically, just as the cold during the late-night ride had not bothered him. Yet he recognized that the heat also had a mental dimension to it, one that he must respect. He was its captive as surely as if it had bound him in chains. He knew, too, that he must contradict the heat's captivity in order that it not oppress him in his soul and spirit. To relieve the heat's oppression, he turned his mind again to his brother's long letter.

~

What exactly are we reading when we read the King's text, my brother? The words are indeed his. The King's text enables us to *hear his voice out of Heaven.* We have much knowledge, as do many of our friends. Yet knowledge of the King's words is what matters. I know something of you, friend, because I know something of myself. We once searched for meaning and purpose away from the King, less regional and ethnic, less historical, and not so ancient. Our sources were also less numinous, not raising in us any awe over the King's design. Our intellect did not enlighten us but instead only made us proud. We pursued the systematic and abstract, overlooking the detailed history of the King's text. We searched for things beyond the great text's regional and ethnic character, tribal faction seeming too messy to carry truth. We lost sight of the hidden King. Then the King *set it all out before us,* the whole secret but spectacular plan of history. He broke into history, revealing himself on the pages of his own text.

Even as he did so, he made his plan just slightly less than obvious, to give a way out to those who wanted to reject him. He told stories, even as he *brought out into the open things hidden since the world's first day.* Those who heard his parables wondered aloud why he did not teach with greater directness, just as people today seek technical answers to spiritual questions. Just when one of his figures asked for a rule or philosophy, or a satisfying incantation, the King instead responded with a telling question or parable, to *create readiness, nudge people toward receptive insight.* He is the master at reading people, using just the right words for each person. When they yearn for formulas, he offers himself as truth. They desire philosophic knowledge. He gives them personal knowledge, which is the only kind of knowledge having truth.

What we read of the King's courage, that he allowed soldiers to nail him to crossed beams, presents a greater challenge to modern readers. The thought is *sheer silliness to those hellbent on their destruction.* Having no stomach for the King facing down death, they have no desire to read his text, which first foreshadows and then describes his great act. When Moses *put a snake on a flagpole* that the dying who looked at it would live, his action anticipated the King on the beams. When we look toward what the King did, we live. Soldiers nailed people to beams to bring deadly shame. The King who had no shame turned shame on its head when he took to his beams. He turned the worst of our devices, torture really, into the best of him, which is just like the King. For such a great act, he has every right to be *named the Jealous One*. What more could anyone do?

Modern readers look for something less powerful and more palatable. They look instead to all sorts of secular priests, experts in cosmology, astrophysics, and other fields. While their parents had looked to the creator King, *another generation grew up that didn't know* him. Their writers attempt to describe the origin, nature, and destiny of man and universe. They profess the goal to reduce all natural laws, forces, and conditions, including time, space, energy, and mass, to a single equation. They act as if we should find guiding counsel in so-called super-string theories of genius minds. While their formulas function, the world treats their associated musings as if they were sacred texts. Those musings become background for entertainment, culture, and literature, supplanting the King's text.

Equations will never inform us like the King's personal knowledge, my brother. Light-speed relativity of mass to energy and space to time are elegant curiosities, evidence of the King's design. Yet we draw no purpose from them. They hold no hope or solace for us. They tell us nothing of human motive or condition, love or hate, war or peace, even of how to conduct a marriage or raise a child. They do not help us come to grips with the death of a parent or friend. We wanted to tell them about someone who could really help, tell them about the King. *We wanted to talk, but they were always too busy.* We appreciate their insight. The universe's magnificent order fascinates us just as it does others. We applaud scientists' efforts for the opportunity it gives us to marvel at the King's creation. We *take a long and thoughtful look* at what the King has created to learn of his power and majesty.

Philosophy, psychology, sociology, and even economics might seem richer ground for us than astrophysics. We have read there, too, and what we read informed us as to their theories. Yet did the existentialist make our hands any softer on the fevered brow of a sick relative or our voices any gentler toward our spouse? They multiply knowledge. Experts abound. Where, though, in any of intellectual school have they found the King's heart? No contemporary philosophy sets our hearts afire with compassion. None hasten us into our poorest neighborhoods and overcrowded jails, as the King does. Theories have no power, while his *fire of love stops at nothing, sweeping everything before it.*

The King spoke to us as he did, knowing what we need to hear. He *picked us out as his from the very start.* He gave us a historical record so rich and sound that we have mined it profitably for millennia. His text works today as readily as in the fourth century. The King fashioned history, posed questions, and provided answers in perfect counterpoise to today's reductionism. His text struck the perfect balance in its antiquity, longevity, and universal application. What he *says goes and stays, as permanent as the heavens.* We substitute nothing contrarily modern for it. We read the King's text.

Indeed, we have the privilege today of reading the King's text in different versions. Our choice influences how often and how well we read. We don't have to *read between the lines or look for hidden meanings.* We choose versions to encourage us in our reading. We avoid as unappetizing cheaply bound hotel versions. As novices, we chose accessible versions. As sophisticated readers, we choose complex versions. Those who say that they do not understand the King's text are probably reading the wrong version. They need a version conducive for novice readers. The child who is unable to draw back an adult's bow never learns to shoot the arrow. *Milk is for beginners, solid food for the mature.* The immature should find a version of the King's text that they can read easily—maybe soft leather-bound with larger print all the way across the page, chapter introductions and life applications.

Veteran readers of the King's text might find editor introductions and life-application footnotes distracting, while those same features support and even enthrall novice readers. Without that help, novices may read without *understanding what they're reading.* Some versions of the King's text are purely to open eyes. We each have our own relationship with the King. The point is that we take time and make effort to select appropriate versions. Think of things most personal to us such as home, car, or clothing. How much time do we spend finding and fitting those things? We should take comparable time and make comparable effort over the King's text. When we resist one version, we should try another, just as we would with ill-fitting clothing. Surely you, my brother, have familiar and comfortable things you value, as did the apostle Paul—perhaps a *winter coat, books, and notebooks.*

When they do not find the King's text conducive, frustrated readers should talk to those who know the text best. We all turn to experts in other fields. Why not do so with the most essential? Experts started reading the King's text where everyone starts. They will have found supportive and accessible versions, and know who reads which versions. An expert reader who is also a friend may know something about the novice reader that would help in choosing the right edition. Our mental, emotional, and spiritual conditions vary. Knowledge of the reader's condition gives the expert more insight into who should read which version. They should not give up their pursuit, my friend. Rather, let them seek wise counsel. *Buy wisdom, buy education, buy insight,* is what they should do.

Occasional readers may have an equal feel for how best to respond to the novice's discouragement. They know the accessible versions. They are sometimes the first to discover a new one. They also know how to get into the King's text from the easiest entry points. Anyone who reads the King's text richly may help others, *sending the misdirected in the right direction.* Versions are not everything. Meaning is always in the history and text. A reader does not need a new edition to grasp additional meaning. Yet a new reader may need that support and inspiration of an accessible edition.

On the other hand, my brother, we need not choose one and only one suitable version. Different versions serve different needs and circumstances. Frequent readers may use several versions of the King's text at once, reading some continuously while making occasional but helpful reference to others. We mark some with notes and highlights while leaving others pristine. Have you followed that practice, my dearest Memphis? I have seen how deeply you draw from texts. If we acquire a version that does not suit us, or hold a version that we outgrow, then we give it to someone who finds it useful. The message remains the same no matter the version. The King does not change in the way that we change. His words remain the same, no matter how we regard them. The King is not *given to lies and changing his mind.* Instead, he promises and then comes through.

The King's text also has many different translations, even within our own language. The translation does not interfere with our reading. Translations differ in connotation. Yet those differences are small compared to the difference between the King's text and any other writing. If one translation is difficult, then we read another. While some hold certain translations in high esteem and claim special inspiration from them, we receive humbly the King's word in any form. We do not argue about translations, lest we *turn our language into babble.*

Translations simply have different uses. Modern usages were common when scholars translated an early version into our own language. Those scholars nonetheless used high-sounding, archaic language to create a more dignified sound for public reading. Public reading requires a different voice, just as Ezra read the text aloud to the remnant. Dignified translation sets the text apart from the many other things we read today. We recognize that peculiar language because we read nothing else like it. We remember its words for the same reason, especially its attractive peculiarities not found in other translations. If instead we need the King's words most like our own, then we have available several other translations. The King's words were not archaic when he spoke them, just as his words remain alive today. Their meaning *isn't too much for us, not out of our reach.* We keep the King's words on our tongues and in our minds as if they were our own.

You are an explorer, though, my dear Memphis, no tourist but intrepid, even courageous in rugged terrain. Other translations offer us those welcome challenges. One version amplifies alternative translations all at once, focusing on each passage's context. That complex version helps us see the text's subtlety and nuance. The King spoke in another language. Our language, which has many more words than ancient languages, can represent most of his words fairly. Yet we can miss in the translation meaning that the King's context and language implied. Juxtaposing alternative translations allows us to comprehend the original meaning. We care that deeply, my beloved brother, to seek the King's every nuance. The King's language had multiple words for crucial concepts like love, whether sentimental, filial, romantic, or sacrificial. We benefit knowing the multiple kinds of love. We see other shades of meaning. Complex versions slow us into developing a greater appreciation for the King's rich and precise meanings. We must *guard the treasure he gave us.*

Other versions modify rather than translate the King's language. Their purpose is not literal but interpretive, to convey to us the same meaning as the ancient text did to its original readers. Those new editions seek to produce the same impact on us as the ancient text had on its original readers. All must be cautious when translating the King's word, lest we alter his meaning. We must not *add to the words or subtract from the words* when it comes to discerning their meaning. While we lack the expertise to judge which version conveys the King's meaning most accurately, we appreciate the value of literal, amplified, and interpretive translations. We do not hesitate to read multiple translations, especially when we fail to understand the translation that we are reading. When information inundates us, we do not let the many versions and translations become obstacles to our reading. We do not hesitate over any translation or edition but instead pick up the nearest. How *blessed the readers, hearers, and keepers of his oracle words.* Our time is so near.

We do not labor at reading. The King created us to reflect on his words. We among all of his creatures possess unique capacity to examine our circumstances. We reflect through an unending internal dialogue with ourselves. We live inwardly, drawing our actions out of our thoughts, our thoughts from our hearts. What *comes out of the mouth gets its start in the heart.* Given our capacity to reflect, we can shape the content of our reflection through selective reading. The ease with which we read influences the frequency with which we read. The version of the King's text that we choose should be as natural as we can make it. Natural form and familiar language simulate our internal dialogue, supplying comfortable and accessible external prompts. We choose versions comfortable to the hands, font familiar to the eyes, translation familiar to the mind, thus reading long and easily. We choose what we favor, as what we favor chooses us. The King knows our hearts. He *knows everything we're going to say before we even start.*

Design counts. We appreciate a book of beauty. Some versions format the King's songs and poems as prose, while others print songs as songs, poems as poems, and prose as prose. Some editions are hardbound, others paperback, and others leatherbound. Leather lasts longer and can be more comfortable resting in the hand for long readings. Some editions use paper so thin that you see the text from the other side of the page, making reading harder. On the other hand, thicker paper makes the text heavier. Heavy texts tend to stay on the shelf. Make reading easier. Love it rather than labor. Best intentions aside, we are creatures of comfort and habit. If the text looks good to the eye and feels good in the hand, then we are more likely to read it. We should *stay at our post reading, giving counsel, teaching.*

We also enjoy the King's text using e-readers and smart phones. Free applications make the King's text a thumb's stroke away. Applications offer conveniences like searching, highlighting, and book marking. We have no reason to avoid technologies that bring the King's text to us more frequently. We have every reason to use them. Anyone with a smart phone can have the text at the fingertips. These conveniences fill our days with his rich words, keeping *each day brimming with his beauty.*

Some versions offer less than the King's full text, perhaps only the newest part. We should not make an incomplete text our only or main text. Although we may not often read some parts, all parts inform the whole. We study the whole of the King's text, while *people who try other ways get nowhere.* The King's text has held form since the fourth century for good reason. If we read only a version that omits portions, then we miss important history and context, and useful material. We *live by every word that comes from* the King's mouth.

Other versions offer more. While I know how astute a student of text you are, my brother, we need not discover on our own the King's text's internal consistency and cross-reference. Annotated versions help us make those connections. Both new and experienced readers use cross-reference to explore and confirm the text's consistency. We use annotations to appreciate its allegory. The text has no equal in its integration and cohesion. The King does not contradict. The King's *words are pure words, refined in fire.* Other versions include time lines, charts, maps, and lists. Theme versions reach men, women, youth, teens, extremes, seekers, and missionaries. Other versions offer life application and spiritual renewal. Each version reaches different readers, filling us until we *pour it out to the King, shaping the river into words.* We can even offer the King's text under attractive cover for readers who judge books by the cover.

Another version reorganizes the King's text chronologically. Inspiration mixes with the history that produced it. Different portions describe the same events from slightly different perspectives, side by side in the chronology. We see new nuance. We also see the full march of history, how *starting from scratch, he made the entire race.*

Other versions offer word and subject indexes so that we can trace the mind of the King. We know the power that words and concepts have to influence us. We know the power of our internal dialogue to shape our attitudes and, accordingly, our lives. Indices help us recall the right words and attitudes. We locate certain passages, key words, and text related to critical concepts. If we are anxious, then an index helps us learn that a *cheerful word picks up the worried heart* and not to get *worked up about what may or may not happen.* We are instead to *live carefree before* the King who cares for us. We gain confidence that we can find the instruction that we need when we need it. We should be thankful for the labor of those who have made reading the King's text so much more productive.

The insight of others can help us understand the text. Some versions annotate the text with detail about the King's ancient societies including their histories, people, and practices. Others annotate with related stories of modern individuals and peoples.

Some versions index annotations so that we can locate detail about the King's people and places. We use the annotations to help us with specific issues. They do not alone give us the King's full story. Reading only what we think we need may help us, like a diagnostic manual. Yet if we do not read the full text, we miss the King's full impact, his *wondrously powerful and transforming present words and deeds* that keep triggering their appropriate response in us.

So yes, brother, we should read what the King's text says about anxiety when we are anxious. We may find prompt relief. Yet to overcome the tendency to anxiety, we must understand its causes and effects, and thus grasp the power and authority the King has given us over it. We must see that power and authority at work in the King's events. We must see for instance how his Spirit strengthened Stephen at the moment of his death, so much that Stephen could pray for his murderers, *don't blame them*. We must recall that Stephen's intercession led to Saul's miracle conversion. We do not find the word anxiety in Stephen's story. A concordance would not lead us to the story. Yet the story demonstrates the power the King gives us over the most anxious situations, to turn those situations into moments of victory in faith. We learn that we must *stand in faith, or you won't have a leg to stand on.*

These demonstrations have value, my brother. Our role is to know the King's words, thank him for good, praise his glory, talk about his work in our lives, and by doing so lift others out of anxiety and depression. Let others believe that circumstances justify anxiety and depression. The King's text has example after example of persons limited in capacity to face even small challenges. Yet after receiving the power of the King's Spirit, they survived with assurance trials that we could hardly imagine. The Spirit's power turns crises into victory. Opponents ridiculed, beat, lashed, imprisoned, and nearly murdered Paul, whose skill was not as a soldier but rather as a tentmaker and scholar. Paul was at *death's door time after time.* Yet he won in every one of those situations. We should not miss the depth of the Spirit's power by reading only single verses specific to our peculiar situations.

So, my friend, we should read the King's text, and the whole text. A frequent reader may have on hand a particular annotated version, for instance a life application or study version, to understand certain characters, events, and passages. The same reader will carry a lighter version without annotations. We do not *pass it off as just one more opinion but take it to heart as* the King's true word. When we read it often in the way we should read it, we find true Jeremiah's experience that we simply cannot restrain it. The King's words are like *fire in our belly, a burning in our bones.* As we read, the King's words burn ever stronger within us until they burn away that which keeps us from him and his loving work.

While we read for ourselves, we see how others receive and live out the King's message. Effective readers read other things at the same time as they read the King's text. Doing so encourages us in our text reading. Writers write a lot about the King's text, more than any other book. Much of that writing helps us read the King's text. A huge literature comforts and encourages us around the King. We read of joy in the hand of sorrow, hope in the grip of despair, and confidence in the face of fear. Some readers complete the King's text, then read a separate text, and then return to reading the King's text. Others read the King's text while simultaneously reading other material. What do you think, Memphis? Should we prefer the latter so as not to have any extended period away from the King's own words? We do not want to lose the Spirit's power and so invite error. We want instead to *take in the extravagant dimensions* of the King's love. Reading the King's text daily keeps in mind knowledge of his love.

We share due caution, my friend, concerning writings about the King's text. Man's work is not always the King's work. For example, one book purporting to be the King's biography so twists the text as to attribute mean-spirited arbitrariness to the King. That author traces the King's mean spirit to pagan gods of the day and vicinity. In doing so, the author fails to distinguish creation's King from his creatures' creations. The author distorts truth with such high style that pundits call his book witty and brilliant. Witticism is apt praise for a badly misguided work because in witticism we err starkly. The author forgets that the King is first, last, and *everything in between*. People have been defaming and rejecting the King forever. We have no need to read books that criticize and condemn the King, to know the extent of others' error. For ages, people have *gone off and betrayed* the King. When they do, they have no one to save them.

Brilliant authors manufacture contradiction out of the King's text by rejecting what the King says about himself. Doing so makes no sense. They cannot judge a thing fairly by first rejecting what it says. They should judge the text by what it says, in which case they would find no contradiction. The King's *revelation is whole, pulling us together.* When we do as the King's text says, which is to construe it as consistent, we see the King's correct attributes. Only by rejecting the King's principle, in other words by violating the text, can they make the King appear contradictory and man brilliant. The King makes wise we who accept him and makes foolish the brilliant who do not accept him. The King's lifts the humble. We find more wise counsel in the King's simple truths that the humble state plainly, than in opposition's brilliance.

Would it be possible to recognize and accept the King by reading and following something other than his text? Could they find his truth in philosophy or mysticism? Their culture suggests that they would find the same god in any wise saying or tradition. Popular belief would have any religious system serving the same function in similar manner. Popular belief, though, is not rational. They have not studied the thing. They do not know the teachers, traditions, and philosophies that they encourage us to follow. Their naiveté is alone enough for us to reject their counsel. They are a *nation of ninnies, not knowing enough to come in out of the rain.* The King is obviously different in his claim, historicity, aim, and accomplishment. Anything goes is not the same as personal knowledge of the King and his uniquely historical faith.

We take a different path, the King's way. We *stick with what we learned, sure of the integrity of our teacher.* We know that every part of the King's text is *useful one way or another.* Those experts who have studied philosophies and religions, really studied them, know the difference. They confirm what you and I know, Memphis, that the King stands alone at the crossroads of history, geography, and humanity. He executed perfectly a frankly miraculous mission. He changed things fundamentally and forever. We see the truth. We know that no other teaching substitutes for his teaching. We may study others. Yet popular opinion does not sway us into thinking that he has any substitute. We find nothing in the latest spiritual fads. To follow those things would be a fatal mistake.

Even books by the King's own professed followers can mislead, my brother. The times influence even the most cautious authors. Material prosperity so blesses us, and mass marketing of that prosperity so influences us, that popular authors today are particularly susceptible to two errors. The first error magnifies our own works rather than to magnify the one true author. The back covers of books written by popular authors tout these books as instant classics. We know, like Martin Luther knew, that to see too much merit in one's own work and to seek the adulation for it is to head straight for hellfire. Rather than thinking *we did all this, we think again.* We know that the King gave us wealth and wisdom, even if we worked for some of it. Without him, we could do nothing. With him, well, anything is possible.

Authors today make a second error, which is to see the King's blessing as burden. Authors assure us that bad news outpaces good news. They portend busy and anxious lives, when in fact we have more security, liberty, and prosperity than any society ever. They tell us what our hearts want to hear, describing us as innocent people who have only made mistakes, as if the King need not have rescued us. They want to *drag us off into endless arguments that never amount to anything.* Yet the King's text speaks truth. They are not innocent, my brother. Their error is not happenstance but the product of their self-pitying nature. Their self-pity deceived them into ingratitude. When they reject the King and instead count their burdens and testify to their miseries, they head for hellfire, while the King blesses us.

We may or may not find our life stories in contemporary books about the King. We do find our life stories in the King's text, where we also find the King. When we read the King's text consistently, we do not have to listen for his gentle whisper. He instead shouts to us. *Everything on earth is his.* Everything we have comes from him. He has all the power and strength, everything that we need. No one holds any power that he does not grant them. When we listen to others, we do so at our peril. They may be saying the things that we want to hear. The notorious Ahab wanted to listen to those sycophants who were trying to buy his favor. When Ahab heard instead from the King's prophet Micaiah, Ahab learned of the disaster that Ahab's idolatry would soon bring.

The King requires loyalty. *If you leave him, he'll leave you,* and the result will not be pretty. Watch for those who will lie to you to get their way with you. They are dangerous, especially when we mistake them as wise. You can always tell them, the moment they step away from the King. We prefer the King's word over any other, no matter in what guise competing authors approach us. The King *says what he means and means what he says.* We measure carefully any other author and reject any contrary message. Everything we read other than the King's text, we read with an eye toward the commitment and intentions of its author. The

King long ago warned us to *get out of this sick and stupid culture.* We allow the King's text to guard us against the peculiar corruptions of our generation. Some contemporary authors call things fundamental principles when they are instead passing fancies and fundamental errors. Without the King's text, few of us can readily tell the difference.

One safer way to read secondary material about the King and his text is to read old material. Most of what we publish today will disappear in no time. Time binds its message to the passing moment. Writing that survives for 100 or 200 years may have something of value, having withstood the test of time. Its errors should also be more evident to us, less likely concealed by today's thinking. Yes, my brother, read what we write today because it speaks to current conditions, but read other material that has withstood the test of time in order to see our errors of contemporary thinking. Above all, read the King's text, which has no such error. We should *stay strong and steady, obediently doing everything written* in the King's text.

Those older reliable writings include John Bunyan's *The Pilgrim's Progress* (1554), rooting itself so deeply in our thought that we still unconsciously use its images. They include Saint Augustine's *Confessions* (325), admitting our condition so needing the cleansing of the King. Albert Simpson's *The Holy Spirit* (1895) shows the allegorical meaning hidden in the King's rich types and figures. Rudolf Otto's *The Idea of the Holy* (1923) identifies our numinous King as the one true Spirit throughout the world. Blaise Pascal's *Pensees* (1670) shows a brilliantly critical mind embracing the reality and urgency of the King's faith. G.K. Chesterton's *The Everlasting Man* (1924) sets world history within its proper context around the King. Francis De Sales's *Introduction to the Devout Life* (1608) shows a life lived day to day with the intimate detail of faith. Brother Lawrence's *The Practice of the Presence of God* (1690) shows how one can walk with God through myriad and mundane details of life. C.S. Lewis's *Mere Christianity* (1943) shows the ultimate reality of the King's heaven.

We have a treasury from which we all do well to draw. Others can help us read the King's text productively, as Ezra helped the remnant of Israel *from the first day to the last.* The King does not always explain all of his text. When Ezra read to the people, he also instructed them at the same time. He *translated so they could understand it and then explained the reading.* Explanation turned the people from weeping to joy at the King's words. We do not let secondary texts draw us away from the King but rather toward him and deeper into his text. We do not cite these teachers or their writings as authority. We find it hard to judge the depth of their insight and extent of their gifts. Only the King's text is authoritative.

We may draw multiple meanings from certain passages. The King's Spirit may lead us to different applications from the same text, depending on our own circumstance. While imprisoned in Herod's jail, John sent disciples to the King to ask the King if he was the one they were to follow. Some readers interpret John's action as seeking reassurance. John may indeed have doubted while in prison and about to suffer beheading. The King's response, naming miracles he had performed while acknowledging John as his herald, encourages those who doubt. The King told the disciples to return to report to John. Yet others might wonder why John would doubt at any time, even in prison, when John had baptized the King in the Jordan River and seen the Spirit like a *dove descending, come down on him.* John heard God's voice recognize the King as his son. So, when the imprisoned John sent the disciples to the King, he may not have been doubting but doing as he should, which was to continue to herald the King.

Our role today, dear Memphis, is like John's role, to send others to the King, not in doubt for their reassurance but in confidence. John intended that we each go to the King for truth.

Once the King received the Holy Spirit, John's role was no longer to tell people that the King was the one to follow but rather to send them to the King. John would have been remiss if he had not sent his disciples to the King and had kept their allegiance. John was right that the King must *move into the center, while we slip off to the sidelines.* Good teachers send students to the right persons and places for the right answers. Because he was in prison about to die, John had to send his students away. What better question could John have given them, than the question whether the King was the one to follow? Our answer to that eternal question determines our rescue. John knew that he must turn his disciples to the King for the answer.

As we read the King's text, dearest brother, let us not let others' instruction steal insight that the King's Spirit gives us. We do not rebuke our teachers or argue over meanings. We listen carefully to teachings. We then read the King's text for ourselves to learn the message he gives us. We can always trust the King's text. Nothing has supplanted or will supplant it. The King's text needs no supplement or updating. The King was right, once and for all. We *don't second-guess him.* We only need to read his text deeply and often. We reject any other text or teaching that discourages that reading. The King has but one way to him, and that way is his way. We do not mistake that anything other than the King's words can show us that path. We have only one King. *At that time I told them, "Get rid of all the vile things that you've become addicted to. Don't make yourselves filthy with the Egyptian no-god idols. I alone am God, your God. But they rebelled against me, wouldn't listen to a word I said. None got rid of the vile things they were addicted to. They held on to the no-gods of Egypt as if for dear life. I seriously considered inflicting my anger on them in force right there in Egypt. Then I thought better of it. I acted out of who I was, not by how I felt.*

The new resident had walked a while longer after the King's departure before stopping to rest in the cup of a small hill covered in soft grass. Rest, though, hardly described the resident's experience. He luxuriated as he reclined in the soft grass, which seemed to catch and embrace him. Every blade caressed him as he laid his head in the grass. His thoughts of the King melted imperceptibly into thoughts of the wife whom for so long he had loved so dearly in the Spirit of the King. He began to dream of his wife, or so he thought. Then he realized that she stood in front of him at the edge of the path. The apparition he had thought to be a dream was instead his wife.

His momentary confusion one could understand, for he was still adjusting to the paradise's unmitigated splendor. As she stood before him, his wife was as earth had barely allowed him to imagine her. She at once had the appearance of youthful health and vigor mixed perfectly with the richness and maturity of age. Her perfection lent no hint of her actual age. She was the wife neither of his youth nor of his old age. Yet he recognized fully the divinity of her perfect form and perfectly peaceful demeanor. Her ideal now perfectly fulfilled had been the divine reason he had asked her to marry him. That divine essence of which he had always known now radiated fully from her every subtle and perfect dimension. Her beauty at once both annihilated and revived him.

He rose instantly without thought or effort to stand before her. They each reached both hands gently toward one another in perfect mirror image until they grasped one another's hands, though still standing apart. He seemed to drink or breathe her beauty, even as he sensed her own immersion in him. Nothing more passed between them than this long look into one another's eyes. They had no need of smile, tears, or embrace. Yet in due time, the moment arrived when each had in silent contemplation simultaneously received all of which each had need and given all each had to offer. That moment arrived just as the King himself arrived. Their hands parted. The King stepped between them. They then turned down the path together, each taking the hand of the King who walked between them.

They did not walk long before the King turned the wife's attention to a beautiful small farm in a broad valley deep below the hillside path. The King's gesture conveyed wordlessly to the new resident and his wife that the new resident had supplied the farm for her. At the King's gesture, both new resident and wife bowed deeply. They then kneeled together before the King, lowering their heads in blissful submission, even while holding one another's hand. When they looked up, the King was gone. The broad valley and beautiful farm lay below them. They rose to begin their descent down the path toward the farm. Their steps grew gradually quicker as they anticipated reunion with the small familiar figures they now saw in the distance around the farm.

What

4

When

He could not discern either the character or intent of the dark figures he saw ahead in the deepening twilight. Yet he sensed danger in their approach. He had faced danger often on his journeys. Two or three times, his life had plainly hung in the delicate balance of an inhabitant's will and intent. Journeys require passage. Passage often requires inhabitant consent. Inhabitants have frequent reason to fear and resist passing strangers. They also often have need or other motive to profit from strangers' passage or indeed to profit from preventing passage. As these figures approached, the traveler had ever-stronger conviction that his passage was presently at substantial risk.

The camels came to an abrupt halt, he thought at the signal of his desert guide. He leaned over in his saddle to look for the guide, presumably hidden ahead of one of the other camels. He wanted to judge the guide's own evaluation of the situation. Yet he saw no sign of the guide. The camels' nervous shifting as the figures drew closer confirmed for him that the guide had disappeared. The guide's disappearance further confirmed for him the approaching figures' ill character and intent. He would face this dangerous encounter alone, he realized with a substantial dose of misgiving. Just for a moment—but only for a moment— his mind recalled the confidence his brother's letter had so far shown in divine protection. He would need it, he thought, smiling briefly to himself at his subtle invocation.

A shot rang in the twilight, causing the camels to jump in place and then skitter. He regretted that he had not noticed any of the figures taking aim at him. Presumably, one had hidden the gun within a cloak. He let himself slump over and slide off his camel's saddle, feigning injury or worse. His unburdened camel ambled off with a confused look. From his vantage point lying still in the sand, he watched for the figures' further approach. His mind culled alternative actions from his training and experience. No one approached. More time passed than he judged reasonable under what he had assumed were the circumstances. Maybe the shot had not come from the twilight bandits. The thought emboldened him to turn his head slowly so that he could scan the horizon behind him.

A figure leading a camel approached. It was the guide. The traveler rose from the sand. He stood still as the guide walked up and handed him the camel's rope with a hint of irritation. No words passed between them. The guide simply turned and headed off, apparently to retrieve their other camels. Then it dawned on the traveler. The guide had shot to scare off the twilight bandits. The traveler's gambit of feigning injury or worse had been unnecessary, costing the guide the effort of retrieving one more camel. He mounted the camel and surveyed the distance for any sign of the bandits. Seeing none, he coaxed the camel to follow the receding guide whose dark figure headed in the direction of their two distant camels.

The traveler's mind turned back to the moment when he had subtly invoked the protection of his brother's beloved divinity. Some wondrous divinity, he thought, one who works quickly, effectively, and in the strangest of ways. He smiled again to himself at the retrospective humor of the event, even as he began thinking of ways to make it up with the guide. Perhaps the guide even thought he had fainted off his camel. The thought made him break into deep laughter. He noticed the guide stop ahead, look back at him, and make a motion with his head that the traveler interpreted as appreciation for (not condemnation of) his laughter. There now, the traveler thought, all is well again, even with the irritated guide. The traveler patted his brother's letter in the backpack strapped to the saddle.

When to read the King's text is right now, my dear brother. No time is like the present. We have no better time to read the King's text than when going about our daily routines eating meals, riding buses, planes, or trains, taking a work break, relaxing after dinner, or in bed at night. We have no better time to read the King's text than when employed or unemployed, in school or on vacation, young or old, rich or poor. *Don't for a minute let this book be out of mind.* It takes you where you are going, making your success. Concerted reading of the same text may seem odd or quaint, but that feeling is only the culture at work. Times have been when persons read the King's text deeply and often. Places are where persons read it at all times. Some people do read it constantly to great effect. Those times, places, and people continue to exist. It works for current and future success, because the King commands it.

One of the text's great tender passages has Moses at the end of his life imploring the King's nation to embrace and share the

King's word at all times. Love the King with all your soul, Moses begs. *Love the King with all that's in you, love him with all you've got.* Keep the King's word on your heart, Moses urges. Impress his words on your children, he implores. Talk about them when you sit at home and when you walk along the road, when you lie down at night, and when you get up, he says. Tie them as symbols on your hands and bind them on your foreheads, in order that they will guide both your thinking and your work, he encourages. Write them on the door frames of your houses and on your gates, in order that you will see them coming in and going out, he directs. Moses knew that for us to live as fully as we can and should, the King's word would need to be everywhere in our lives, not just ceremonially on Sunday but present every day of the week, at all times and in all places.

Right now is also the right time to read the King's text in a different sense. Moses encouraged the nation to attend to the King's word at the end of the nation's 40 difficult years in the desert, just as the nation was about to enter the Promised Land. After directing the nation to read and know the King's word, Moses warned that the Promised Land's milk and honey would distract them from doing so. When you *watch your standard of living going up and up, make sure you don't become so full of yourself and your things that you forget* the King, he warns. The King did so much for the nation, and yet it would forget the King.

The King knew that his people would live in a land of flourishing cities, in houses filled with good things including plentiful drink and food—just as we do. The King foretold that the nation would enjoy the many good things in their fine homes, drink much, and eat the good foods, just as we do. He saw that their satisfaction would lead them to forget the King, just as some of us do. The King *began telling them what was going on before it even happened.* He knew how people think. Troubled and lean times do not threaten them. The complacency that comes with their prosperity is their bane, for in those times they forget the King's word.

As much as we have in the way of material things, my brother, we should especially heed this teaching. Our time to turn to the King's text is not only when danger appears and death lurks. The time to read the text is when prosperity lures us — when the garage, bank account, closet, and day are all full. Prosperity threatens things of eternal value. Material blessings cannot replace a heart for others, our willingness to serve a King vastly greater than ourselves, or our love for that King. Lean times keep us turning to these better things that we know save and protect us. Fat times turn us from them, unless we know enough to read the King's text in time of blessing. His counsel for us in those times is *simple and straightforward: go ahead with what he gives us,* particularly, himself. Live as if he is all that matters. And in those good times, be more thankful than ever.

Prosperity can be a time of great opportunity to make significant changes for the better in our lives and the lives of those around us. Changes are never easier than when good health, firm friends, and stable finances bless us. We think that only crises can change us. We wait for crises to remove our pride and restrict our recreations, like the man who waits for a heart attack to change his diet. Yet if that man still lives, he may have lost his capacity to work and with it lost his job, home, finances, and family. If we read the King's text when blessed, then we may not only avoid disaster but also bring the King's new blessing greater than we had previously imagined. Good life depends on change and transition. Both work better off blessing than failure. The lives of Abraham, Joseph, Moses, and David show the King heaping blessing on blessing when they continued to live in him. *Not once have I seen an abandoned believer.* The King's followers are so generous that they look rich. Even their children do well. In sports and business, they call it momentum. We agree that the King blesses those who pursue his favor.

We should also know our time in history, as the nation of Israel knew its time in its history. The returning remnant used their history to rebuild God's temple. Their former captors let them begin that work, indeed blessed them with the necessary resources, when they learned Israel's history. When scoffers stopped their work with false rumors, the Israelites invoked a historic decree that had freed them from their bondage, to continue the work on the temple. They asked, *Why should the work come to a standstill?* The King is always at work. We too must know our time in history and continue our work mindful of that time. To regain our freedom and make ourselves fit for the King, we must know about the King who freed us. He did it, not us. We gain that freedom through him.

The current narcissistic and sensual culture is good reason for us to read the King's text. Culture is at war with the King, hardening hearts from his love and turning them from his service. In our therapeutic age, they place themselves rather than the King at the center of everything, pursuing their fulfillment over the only one who fulfills, meaning the King. Their spiritual and moral development arrests in narcissistic state. They seek personal gain and satisfaction over corporate and community good in their work and recreation, and even in their relationships. All things, including intimacy itself, they perceive to exist in a market of goods available to the highest bidder. A cold wind blows as they bid themselves out. Many reject even a pretense of civility or scruples. Yet some *make a clean break of their failures* toward the King, in which case he quickly forgives them.

Others with hearts still hardened against the King still somehow desire his fulfilling intimacy. They sense it but have rejected the one who would provide it to them. So they instead pursue sensuality with unprecedented vigor. We know better than *going along with the crowd, an empty-headed, mindless crowd.* Yet they follow right along because they do not see it. They are too far from the King because they made sure not to have any heart for him. Without his intimacy, they instead exhibit unquenchable appetite for food, music, art, sex, theater, travel, technology, and anything else that stimulates their senses. They keep going in deeper and deeper until they *lose touch with reality itself.* They pursue so aggressively those things that stimulate the senses that they spend fortunes seeking the perfect meal and moment, when that kind of perfection is simply not possible.

Dear brother, how careful we must be to avoid this deadly combination of a hard heart that aggressively seeks sensuality. Those who go that way get truly lost. *Bilious and bloated,* they say that the King is dead or unreal. They have totally lost it. The King looks hard to find anyone who really pursues him in the way that he deserves, but the King finds none. We are short of proper pursuit, some of us more than others. The King warns us that he can't stand a hard heart chasing after sensuality. When they lose their love for him and lose his love along with it, they must replace his love with something else. When they lose sensitivity to one another and to the difference between right and wrong, just and unjust, love and hate, they replace it with sensuality, mistaking one for another.

To put it bluntly, they mistake ability to experience and appreciate things sensually, such as a fine sunset, play, or wine, for having a soft heart or sensitive spirit, when sensuality is so different from sensitivity. Now would be the time for them to read the King's text, as they chase after the perfect experience of the perfect beach at the perfect resort destination. We all enjoy good things, but enough is enough, and too much is too much. At least we know when to stop imbibing and to turn to the King. We recognize that time often and take full advantage of it. Reading the King's text is indeed a happy discipline, my friend. We *delight far more in what he tells us about living than we do in piling up riches,* that's for sure. We watch what he says.

Naturally, good reading mechanics increase our reading time and enjoyment. Holding the text up as we read, rather than letting it lie flat on desk or table, save us postural aches and pains in wrists, arms, hands, neck, and shoulders. Propping up the King's text or using a bookstand eases and frees our hands for notes and turning pages. Good light and comfortable seating increase our reading ease and endurance. We should have places in the home where we read regularly and in comfort. If we do not have desk, table, or stand on which to prop the King's text, lamp for good lighting, and soft chair with upright back and arms, then we should acquire them. Imagine that: a home in which we keep a special place for reading about the King. They justify a lot of time, labor, and expense for gardens, recreation rooms, and entertainment centers, when more of us should take the time and make the effort to arrange suitable reading places. They think *it's the right time to live their fine homes* while the King's place goes wanting. They should spend more time and attention on the King.

Peace and quiet are other aids for reading the King's text, we both know, my friend. Reading the King's text around a friend or family member, silently while occasionally sharing insights or aloud in turns, is also smart. Admonishing spouse or child to be silent as we read is not the point. We do not read the King's text to escape or avoid others but to engage them more lovingly. If spouse or child would benefit by our attention, then we give it to them gladly. We are polite when reading the King's text and will put aside reading when we should be giving time and attention to others.

Our sensitivity helps others respect and support our reading. We want them to respect and like it that we read about the King. So to keep the peace, we choose different times to read. We might make that time early morning or late evening, lunch hour at work, or when other family members are occupied in other recreations. We have the time. We need only find it, and when we cannot find it, to make it, while not at the expense of relationships. The King just loves it when we hang out with him rather than *slink along*

Dead-End Road. He loves it when we read and think about his words.

Another helpful practice to increase our reading is to look at what we read instead of reading the King's text. If we simply stop reading weekly magazines about food, fashion, fitness, or whatever other diversion into which we have fallen, we find so much more time to read the King's text. They think the King does not notice when they ignore him in favor of these reading diversions. They think *nobody's tending the store* and that they can get away with everything. And for a while it may work. Then it catches up with them. If they would simply stop reading those parts of the daily newspaper like the advertising, comics, sports, and daily tragedies that add nothing to their lives, then they would find the time to read the King's text and meditate on its passages that renew their hope and vigor. If they eliminate the detective novels, then they suddenly find themselves with hours to read about and reflect on the King's mystery.

See, we stick with the King because *he's all we've got left.* And we are not sad. We would want no other. He keeps waking us up every morning. When we pursue the King, truly pursue him, we find ourselves gradually relieved of great amounts of useless and often frankly harmful thinking. He *gives us a map* that takes us to him. We find that map in his text. It just takes some time to sit down with it and read it.

They shouldn't think we are kidding. Imagine them left on a deserted island with only the last newspaper, magazine, or novel that they just read. Their isolation would condemn them to read it over and over. That drudgery would be an unfortunate fate, wouldn't it? Yet that fate is close to what they choose when they do not consider carefully their reading. They pick up new issues of newspapers or magazines each week, but the stories are pretty much the same over and over. After 20 or 30 years of these habits, they should realize that they have been reading the same depressing stories. Only the names and dates change. They read nothing but what depletes, distracts, and hurts them. They should read something redeeming instead—the King's text. *Huge in mercy*—that's the King. He makes it all right.

When we reach the end of the King's text, we start right in again. We can do that because its meaning is inexhaustible. Reading the King's text once does not mean that we have finished it, although some treat it that way. Instead, each reading lends us new insight. A first reading is like an exploration. The King's terrain seems at once familiar and foreign. The King dominates the text in a way that is fully foreign to those who think little of a creator king. The thoughts and actions of his text's historical figures seem to spring from our own frightened and confused interiors. A second reading we still find uncertain, although the King's exquisitely powerful nature stands out in greater clarity. His *thundering breakers seem to crash into and crush us.*

Subsequent readings bring new revelation of the King's character. Fitting the text's teachings into our active thought—into our constant internal dialogue—may still seem unusual in a third reading. Yet we begin to anticipate and even relish reading of now-familiar events, while the words themselves begin to resonate in our souls. The text begins to shape our thinking to signposts and teachings. Those thought patterns become first vaguely or then crisply familiar. A fourth reading gives us a solid timeline, increasing our insight into the text's structure. We develop favorite passages and phrases. Our minds become hungry for the text's inspiration. We find guidance not simply in the King's words but also in his attributes. The text begins to shape our decisions. It helps us respond to specific challenges. The King begins to *validate our lives in the clear light of day.*

Think of these riches, my good friend. A fifth reading shows relationships between different times and events in the King's text. Ancestry, patterns, types, foreshadowing, and other connections between people, places, and events begin to appear to us out of our familiarity with the text. That familiarity helps us see similar connections between different parts of our own lives. A sixth reading reveals broad themes in the text, now easily recognized and often confirmed. The effect is like waking up to reality, that we have this great King. *Wake up you sleepyhead people. King-Glory is ready to enter.* The text clearly now measures our lives, which the text simultaneously guides us, confirming the activity and effectiveness of its themes. A seventh reading shows certain phrases and words suddenly standing out as distinct, sharp, incisive, and fresh. Individual phrases and words now actively shape how we perceive, think, and speak. An eighth reading resolves misunderstandings we had of the text, which now looks even more cohesive and meaning-rich.

We could continue, Memphis, couldn't we? Some mysteries that we discover in repeated readings we must not reveal but instead leave for individual exploration. When the King takes hold of us, we just might, like Paul, be *swept in ecstasy to the heights of heaven*, about which, again like Paul, we would not tell. Such ecstasy is possible, even though we do not in any sense make it our goal. We know, though, that the more we read the King's text, the richer we read it. It has more lasting and profound of an impact each time. It changes how we see ourselves, others, and the design and operation of things around us. The King might then lift us up to paradise, where we too, like Paul, would hear the inexpressible. We do not countenance mysticism. Our end is to honor the King, not to pursue mystical experience. Yet the King holds more for us than that which he reveals to others who read his text only occasionally. The King's *mystery in a nutshell*, though, is simply that the King gets into us until we share in his place. What that is actually like we cannot really speak to one another without spoiling it.

When we reach the end of the King's text, and starting over seems daunting rather than inviting, we consider alternatives. We read select parts of the King's text with a particular theme in mind. We may read Paul's letters with an eye toward how the

King's Spirit works. We then gain new appreciation for his Spirit. For another example, we might read the four parts that each tell of the King's own story, reading for how each person who interacts with the King approaches him, meaning how he reveals each person's motives. That question is our own challenge, to see how we daily relate and respond to the King. For another example, we might read the histories of the older part of the King's text, concentrating on the figures' acts as those acts honor or dishonor the King. We might then see better how our own acts garner his recognition and reward, remembering that although his love is *oceanic, nothing gets lost in his largeness.*

Those who do not read of the King often will complain that they would tire of the practice, even though they might agree that it would be good for them. They might even call it too much of a good thing. They might claim that they are waiting for inspiration. Yet they lose the battle entirely when they imagine the King's word as wearying them. Who wearies whom? They so *quickly tire of him, even though it wasn't that he asked that much of them.* They have it backwards. He does not wear them out with anything. They weary him with their complaining. We could accept wearing ourselves out for the King, although we seldom do so, and he does not really ask us to do so. He never wearies us. They weary him with their foolish offenses. They also weary themselves after their own worthless pursuits. When we tire of the physical part of reading, we do not say to ourselves or tell others that the King's text itself tired us. We recover our physical strength and then read on. We also ask him for strength to renew us. When we *find ourselves flagging, we go over his story again,* giving us the strength we need.

The thing we hope to accomplish is to ferret out each of those little things that keep us from getting closer to the King, even those timing things about when to read his text. We benefit from its reading in every circumstance, whether we are happy or sad, well or in pain, contemplating things or just skimming along the surface. The King's text guides us even when we are in any of those conditions. We read when we are high and when we are low, when we are old and when we are young, at an early fork in our road, at a mid-life change, and at the end of life. Our reading is worthwhile because the King made us to experience him and to experience him through his words. We've *got a good thing going and are not letting go.*

Memphis, we have little need of hearing counsel for the very young. We are young no longer. Fortunately, the King's text is good for the mature and elderly. The King had a hard lesson for Moses at the end of Moses' epic life. No one quite lived such an extraordinary life as Moses. Yet the King had Moses follow his command just like others, even when Moses was ready to honor the King more than those around Moses were ready to give the King honor. In the King's text, we also read of the patriarch Jacob and of David dealing near the end of their lives with the jealousies and succession of their children. We read Solomon's wisdom, hearing from a man who had everything and yet still searched for meaning. The King's text shows how their strengths and weaknesses, and their successes and failures, depended on their relationship with the King, right into old age. What did they do that the King's text teaches us to embrace or avoid, so that we may know at the end that we have lived the right life? Even the thief on the cross next to the King made the right end. No matter how we live our lives, we must still figure out how to end our lives with the assurance that our next breath will be in the King's kingdom. We *plan on looking him full in the face and live heaven on earth.* The King's text tells us how.

The ultimate question, my brother, lies in what we leave behind when our time comes. What legacy will remain of either of us? Will others recall us, and if they do, how will they remember us? The King's text addresses what happens at the end of life. Our lives and actions must honor the King through the love we show others. When the King winnows our words and actions, we must justify all those persons, purposes, events, and other things for whom and for which we lived. Only a residue or aura of us will remain in the memories of those whom we leave behind. Fire burns away chaff, leaving only the roasted kernel of our actions. The fire is the King's fire. Both the King and others will judge us according to the King's standard. It *makes no difference who you are or where you're from.* We all live by the same standard. The King does not show favoritism. Neither do others after our departure. Power, riches, and our ability to pursue those things are gone the moment we die. We ought to know and care deeply about the King's standard, revealed again in the fire of our earthly demise.

The lessons that the King's text teaches the old are also for the younger who still have time. The King can still help them shape their legacy. We can do no better than the King as the pattern for a purposeful life. At early age he knew, stated, and carried out his life's mission. While the master of all, the King yet allowed his Father to define his life's course. He then followed that course with complete assurance. His compassion in doing so accomplished no less than to alter the course for everyone who came after him. The King forever and fundamentally changed, indeed fully described and completed, the possibility of life. He transformed responsibility and opportunity, indeed remade consciousness. We have no better model to follow in every moment of life than the Author and Word of life. His *road stretches straight and true.* Everyone, no matter the time and station in life, can take best counsel from the King, learning from his text the teaching, model, and way of the King.

While the King's text counsels both the old and young, it also serves those who are in the middle, maybe like you, Memphis. We talk about mid-life or a turning point in life, although no one knows the day and hour of their end and parting. The King's text describes figures who start on the right course but lose course later in life, like Saul, Gideon, Hezekiah, and even Solomon. The

King's text also describes figures who start on the wrong course but then find the right course later in life, like the apostle Paul. The King's text also describes the decisions that David made and the consequences of those decisions for David who led the King's nation from early to late in life. The King's text goes so far as to describe David's huge error with terrible consequences in mid-life. In these respects, the King's text has models for facing crises, even crises so serious as to indicate that a person has just thrown away much of the person's life. The King's text also offers models for keeping on course a life already well lived or for adjusting so as to get on course at mid-life. No time is better than the present time to read the King's text, no matter our station and course in life. *Without him, nothing makes sense.*

We do not have to rely on our own reasons for reading. The King's text itself tells us the urgency of its message. Tell me, good brother, isn't our end near, not only for you and me but for all of us? *We all die sometime.* But don't take that statement as fatalism. The King lives to bring us back to him. Sound minds might once have thought the apocalypse a figment of rampant prophetic imagination. The end of something as large and stable as the world seemed beyond the possible. Yet today even the person of no faith other than blind confidence in the material world believes the end of this world possible. Many credible thinkers believe it to be more than possible, even soon if not immediate. It is no longer ridiculous to imagine the world ending. I do not mean here the scientist's imagination that all worlds must obey the laws of thermodynamics and end in a cold, dead state. Rather, I mean our readily apparent ability to extinguish ourselves in nuclear holocaust. I mean also our prospective ability to change the natural environment sufficiently to cause temperatures to increase, waters to flood, deserts to expand, famines to erupt, and atmosphere to disintegrate. I mean also the sudden advent of terrifying new epidemic diseases. Today, only the fool sees certainty in the midst of such extraordinary new dynamics.

Why then is now the right time, my dearest friend, to read the King's text? The answer should be clear now. We have no way of mistaking it. The King's text says that it will be so. The King's text predicts these times. The text foretells that the end will become apparent. I am not making things up. In fact, the King's text urges us to *watch out for doomsday deceivers*. Yet the text also says that the end will come after everyone has an opportunity to read about and receive the King. Aren't we close to that point, my brother? Isn't information more widely available to more people today than at any other time, indeed, more so than we ever imagined? The King's text shows us the panorama of human history from its intimate beginning in the Garden of Eden to its fearsome end in apocalyptic vision. If ever a time existed to read and take to heart the message of the King's text, then now is that time. We can so clearly see that the present peace we have is but an interlude before the final storm and that final storm looms so certain. *I'll reduce Egypt to an empty, desolate wasteland all the way from Migdol in the north to Syene and the border of Ethiopia in the south. Not a human will be seen in it, nor will an animal move through it.*

The new resident and his wife descended the valley to the small farm below. The small figures below stood at the farm's gate watching the pair descend. A pack of the figures finally broke their standstill in favor of a mad dash up the last hill to greet the pair. The dogs rushed up leaping at the wife, each planting a kiss on her cheek in their leap before bounding on to dash in joy around her. The new resident stood back, smiling at the happy melee, watching his wife catch, hug, and release any bounding dog desiring it. Most of the dogs he knew. A few he recognized only from old photographs. All were the picture of perfect health and manners. He smiled again as those he knew each exhibited the unique mannerisms he now recalled associating with them.

His attention turned again toward the farm now a short distance below. Horses, more dogs, and a few cats gathered around a figure, respectfully awaiting his approach. He walked to the gate and swung it open to greet the daughter he and his wife had loved so dearly and long, and who had so blessed them throughout their earthly years. The greeting with his wife had been silent. Not a word had passed between them since they had met. In contrast, the daughter greeted the new resident with a torrent of joy-filled words. She mixed nicknames and terms of endearment in with the remembrances and experiences that she gushed, even as she simultaneously pointed out the dogs' antics around her mother who had joined them at the gate.

They spent the next days catching up with one another while enjoying every animal on the farm, the valley's sunshine and fresh air, and brisk walks among the hills. They met many neighbors with whom they shared gifts from the farm's plenty and from whom they received like gifts. The new resident's wife shared exquisite jewelry, beadwork, and sewn work she had crafted at the farm.   The daughter taught delighted children while organizing public works and other valley ventures. The new resident, though, kept a little to himself, waiting for the King's signal. He knew that he had more of the realm to discover, and more to learn about its residents, before he could call the farm or any other place his celestial home.

Indeed, the King appeared in good time, just as the new resident had anticipated. The new resident had taken his favorite dog up one of the hills to sit and watch the activity on the farm below, while the dog explored the grasses and hillocks around him. The King appeared at the new resident's side, sitting beside him in the grass. The new resident bowed his head in deepest respect and wept, as new residents are wont to do in the kingdom. The King wept with him just as he had when they first met. Then together they watched the activity on the farm below, each pointing out things that they knew and observed about the farm's animal and human inhabitants. The new resident recognized then that the King had long ago shared with him these gifts of observation and discernment.

Their insights ended. The new resident looked at the King, knowing without words that the King had authorized him to embark on his next journey. Confirming what the new resident already understood, the King said simply that he would descend to tell wife and daughter. The new resident and King rose simultaneously, the King smiling once briefly at the new resident before bounding down the hill. The King's smile blinded the new resident, who for an instant felt the glorious expanse of the entire kingdom. When the new resident regained in another moment his sight and senses, he was standing in a different part of the realm surrounded by majestic mountains.

5

Where

He could just see the outline of the ruins ahead in the early dawn. After another night's travels, the guide had left him at the head of the path, indicating that he had an hour's walk to the ruins. The hour had passed quickly as he thought about what would likely be his last adventure. He had seen many ancient ruins on his travels. He realized now that he must have been seeking something more than adventure in these travels. What had drawn him to ruin after ruin? His thoughts about seeking after ruins mixed with reflections on his brother's long letter. His brother, he knew, sought after something, indeed someone, quite different. His brother's living God even spoke against chasing after Egypt's ruins.

His revelation unnerved him briefly. The dawn's outline of the ruins ahead in deepest Egypt now gave him a sense of foreboding rather than anticipation. He continued to hike toward the ruins even as his excitement gave way to something more like regret. Yes, they were thousands of years old, but perhaps still they were simply ruins—and dangerous ones at that. Was this new conscience what his brother's letter would call a leading of the Spirit? The letter pressed on his side through his small day pack as if physically to turn him back, but he shrugged off the thought in favor of reconnoitering his entrance into the ruins.

He saw no one as he passed the first tumble-down walls at the ruins' perimeter. The massive stone walls gradually grew in height and order as he pressed further into the ruins. He stopped for a moment, realizing that he discerned no purpose in his pressing forward. Did the ruins have a center? What did he expect to find? Yet the place drew him forward, to what location or end he knew not. He thus resumed his exploration, having relinquished his purpose to the place itself. The rising walls now darkened his path even as the sunlight above grew brighter. He passed through tunnels and small chambers, running his hand on the wall along the narrowing path to ensure that he followed its contour in the darkness.

One moment he thought that he heard voices ahead. He stopped and called. His voice echoed, but all was silent once again. He thought he saw a flickering light ahead. He resumed his path in the direction from which he thought that he had heard the voices, toward the flickering light. His sense of foreboding grew now with each step. He stopped often, each time preparing to turn back, having now fully realized the aimlessness and danger of his adventure after ruins. Yet he felt as if he could not turn back. He had committed his life to this path of adventure long ago, and the commitment now overwhelmed him. In that moment, he again felt his brother's letter press against his side through the day pack. In response, he said a word of prayer to his brother's God, just at the moment that the painful blow struck his skull from the behind him.

So then, dear brother, where should we read the King's text? One sees a lot of his text in jail. No doubt, jail is a good place for reading the King's text. Jail humbles hearts. Depriving a person of liberty and then making the person depend in every respect on the goodwill of the jailer humble an arrogant attitude. *Set in their ways, they won't change.* And then, bang, jail gives them a new attitude. In jail we see and hear more insightful statements about the King, deeper relationships with the King, and more study of the King than anywhere else, which makes sense. It takes humility. Speaking good of the King, and having a relationship with him, and then reading his text consistently, work miracles among humbled persons. The King loves a humble heart. In jail we find persons who have more of the King's Spirit, clearer understanding of the King's purpose, and stronger desire to do his work.

Jail inmates also more readily admit their need for what the King brings. Funny thing is, others who are not in jail have equal need of the King but deny it. The King's text supplies two resources, comfort and guidance, in abundance. Relationship with the King based reading his text and then doing what it says bring us out of our own figurative prisons. Then the King's text keeps us out. After all, when we find ourselves in those figurative prisons, the King is the *one we violated, and he's seen it all, the full extent of our evil.* Even when we have our literal liberty, we are like those who are in literal jails, in need of the King. Even our favorite figures in the King's text, heroes like Moses, David, and Paul, found themselves in their own desert and cave prisons, and literal jails. *Mighty men of ancient lore, the famous ones,* they still violated the King's standard and thus needed the King's rescue.

True enough, Memphis, neither of us has any expectation of

spending any time in jail other than to visit the prisoner. Yet of course, we should not only read the King's text to stay out of jail. The first and best place to read the King's text is at home. Simply clearing our home of catalogs, magazines, and other distracting writings, putting them out of sight, clears and prepares our minds to read the King's text. We then consider preparing a special place in the home to read the King's text, say, a soft chair by a garden window. We might reserve that place for nothing other than reading of and from the King. The King's Spirit rewards us with special insight when we give the text the recognition it deserves in this manner. He *gave us his good Spirit to teach us to live wisely.* He withholds nothing from us because he wants us to flourish.

Keeping two or three copies of the King's text in handy and visible places around the home makes it more likely that we will read it. We should read the King's text anywhere in the home including not just the office, living room, or den but also the kitchen counter, dining table, and bedroom. We can also read the King's text anywhere around the home, while laying on the deck in the sunshine, sitting in the garage with the door up watching a rainstorm, or waiting on the front porch for family to return home with groceries. This reading is *no small matter for us, it's our life.* Those words are what make us live long and happily. We should make reading the King's text a part of our homes and surroundings. Doing so makes our home a haven, first for us, then for our family, and finally for anyone who enters. The King rewards our reading and loving his words. We find more love, peace, forgiveness, joy, affirmation, and assurance in a home whose inhabitants read the King's text prominently. We hope to see it visible in places around the home.

Home is not the only place to read the King's text. If we keep a copy in our car, we find ourselves reading it on one of those unexpected waits for traffic, passenger, or meeting. We might carry our copy into a meeting place even if that meeting place already has copies available. Doing so enables us to highlight the text, make margin notes, and, when the meeting inspires us, to readily find passages we have already highlighted. We then also have it on hand after the meeting when someone brings up a question. We might also carry it into all sorts of places so that our children or someone else's children notice and wish to imitate us. Carry it around long enough, and you'll be able to say someday, *Now they got it and understood the reading given to them.*

I understand that not all are as devoted to doing the right thing as you, my brother. They may feel embarrassed at first to carry the King's text, especially if no one else is doing so. They may even feel funny to have the text around their home, especially if no one else in the family understands. If they feel too embarrassed to carry a copy someplace, then probably they should examine the place they are going and the commitment of the people they meet there. If they feel embarrassed to carry a copy of the King's text anywhere, then they need to examine themselves. Remember the King's jealousy. Anyone *embarrassed over him and the way he leads them around their fickle and unfocused friends* had better watch out. The King is not going to like that one bit when they meet him. When they are more concerned about how others view them than how the King views them, or how they ought to view themselves, then they are in big trouble. *Don't lie to one another*, they should be thinking. We have put those lies behind us, exchanged them for the truth of the King. For them to live for a self image that the culture imposes on them is to live enslaved. They stand no chance that way.

We think it curious how some would shudder for others to see them kneeling in submission to the King, or asking his favor before a meal at a restaurant, or carrying his text into any public setting other than where lots of people do so. Yet those same persons, whom popular views of appropriateness so define, will wear the most curious clothing and accessories to a gala, or spend hours running about the streets in the most unusual fitness clothing, without giving a second thought to the odd nature of their dress and activities. The King *examines every heart and sees through every motive.* He knows what we want, and he has a way of supplying it to us. Some give no thought to the images that they pursue and the culture that influences them. Instead, they condemn the things that others pursue, even when those things include the King. It's funny because the King is never impractical, bizarre, or silly. He makes such good sense.

The personal cost such popular thinking imposes, that they must conform to fashion while rejecting the King, of which even we are sometimes guilty, is great. The cost is condemnation, and not just anyone's condemnation but the King's condemnation. *As long as they did what they felt like doing, ignoring the King, they didn't have to bother with right thinking.* But that self-pursuit got them nowhere. Instead, it cost them everything, when they lost the King. While they will soon know that all hope is lost, we find the opposite is true. We do not see ourselves resting our head on the pillow knowing we draw our last breath, while thinking of the false things we pursued, and our lost opportunity to serve the King. The King told that very story of the rich man who ended up in hell for having pursued his comfort while ignoring the sick beggar at his gates. The beggar ended up in heaven. The rich man wanted just the slightest taste of cool water but didn't get it. They found a *huge chasm set between them so that no one can go from one to the other even if he wanted to.* The rich man begged to send a messenger back to his living brothers, who would be we, my dear Memphis, urging us to consider our fate. We have already gotten that message. In the King's text, we have all the warning we need. If they will not listen to what the King's text tells them, then why would they obey hell's messenger? Let them be certain that when the end comes, they can say that they followed the King. Let's keep reading the King's text everywhere, so that we do not lose that message.

The modern devices of which we are so fond, my friend,

facilitate reading the King's text. Reader devices give us access to online texts anywhere signal and power reach. We can read on the bus or airliner, before and after meetings, and on work breaks. We can read the King's text while walking and exercising. A few minutes here and there throughout the day add up to substantial daily time reading the King's text, bringing its insight and his Spirit's presence into the midst of our daily activities. The King has been *blessing us in all our work, so let's make a day of it and really celebrate.*

We might at the same time ask where the King's word reaches. Where does it find its effect? Here too lies a mystery of the King's Spirit. We find the effect of the King's words in what many would think the most unlikely of places and people. Some might not think that the King's words could possibly penetrate the corporate boardroom. Yet they do. Corporate executives often take a keen interest in the King's principles. Given their substantial power, corporate executives face the temptations of pride and arrogance even as they bear great responsibility for others. They also face constant challenge and insecurity. Leaders in business, government, the arts, education, social services, and other fields recognize the need to have a foundation for judgments. Because they routinely make such judgments, they have great need for articulating a sound basis from which to judge. The King's text is certainly for leaders and about leaders, even if the popular conception is the opposite that it is mere solace for the downtrodden. One such King-like leader, Queen Esther, learned leadership's imperative. She learned from the King that if you *stay silent at a time like this, help and deliverance* will come from another leader. Sometimes we only get one chance.

Indeed, we know, dear Memphis, that the King's text is about leaders, the lessons of leadership, and the special challenges leaders face. The King's nation installed Joash as its king at the tender age of seven. As long as Joash followed the wise counsel of the chief priest Jehoiada, who was responsible for Joash's coronation, Joash and the kingdom prospered. The priest's counsel was so wise because he *made a covenant between himself and the king and the people.* See, the leaders don't always have to know the King directly. Leadership also prospers when it listens to the counsel of others who commit to the King. Leaders prosper when they remain listeners, guidable and teachable, and when they follow the King's teaching. Joash allowed the chief priest Jehoiada to rid the nation of idols and to guard and protect both the king and the temple from that which would destroy them. They *formed a ring around the young king, weapons at the ready.* Wherever the young king went, he had the counsel of followers of the great King. Sound leaders allow the King's Spirit to inform and protect them in order that they make wise, just, and merciful decisions.

Yet when the wise priest Jehoiada died, Joash did what leaders usually do with the wrong heart and absence of wise counsel, which was to listen to those who buttered him up. *After the death of Jehoiada things fell apart, going from bad to worse.* The pride of leadership is always its downfall. When the King sent prophets to Joash, the young king even stoned one of those prophets, a son of Jehoiada, who had the temerity to condemn Joash's harmful practices. Without the protection of wise counsel, Joash died a disgraceful death. His own officials murdered him after Joash lost a battle to a handful of enemy soldiers who had killed all the other leaders of his people. Bad leadership has its consequences. Bad leaders are losers, destroying their followers and squandering resources.

Over and over, the King's text has the right lessons for leaders like us, my dear Memphis—and I do call us leaders. Our challenge is not so much to recognize the need for a foundation or even to recognize the King's text as the right source. Leaders are often quick to appreciate the power, clarity, and purpose behind the King's teaching. When the King's message *came to us, it wasn't just words. Something happened in us.* It gave us incredible conviction. So instead, our challenge is to break down the barriers to reading and talking about that conviction. The same corporate and community leaders who speak privately about right service and action, and the King's love and mercy, sometimes hesitate to do so publicly. The King's words too often remain at the edges of the corporate and community consciousness or just outside of it where his words can do no good.

We also find the King's text in places where we rarely think of leadership or power—yes, in jails and prisons, but also in hospitals and factories, and among the homeless. Here also we find the power of the King's words to lift up, lift out, heal, comfort, provide, and persevere. Professionals like doctors, nurses, lawyers, and counselors who serve the powerless draw special purpose from the King's text. The text tells professionals that the King wants them to *break the chains of injustice, get rid of exploitation in the workplace, free the oppressed.* The text tells them that the way to have their own light rise is not to do things for show but to do those things that actually serve the poor. The King does not like show. In fact, he hates it when they do things for their own reputation. He loves the real action that serves others who need it. When followed, the King's words transform both the powerless and those who have the skills and resources to serve them. No place is beyond the reach of the King's words. We find no social class or position that his words cannot touch. We feel his power in all places equally, if we let him be our consciousness. Reading the King's text is for people in all places.

Reading the King's text has yet another place to it, dear brother, and that place is the place that we need to be to receive the benefits of reading. To receive the King's lessons, we must start with simply reading them. We must pick up the text and read. Yet what we receive from reading depends on where we are when we read, meaning that it depends on how prepared we are to read effectively. We must prepare ourselves, or let the King's Spirit prepare us, to allow the words to soak into our consciousness. It is not enough to just let the words pass before our eyes and out of our minds as we quickly as we scan them. We must allow the King's Spirit to prepare us to receive and accept the King's teaching. He *sticks by those who stick with him.* He does not stick with those who are already stuck up on themselves. We must be in the right frame of mind to receive the King.

Let us acknowledge, dear Memphis, that a reader unprepared to accept the King's teachings, one who reads them only to put them on trial challenging each premise, will not receive the King's teaching. They can reject anything. The unprepared can easily misunderstand, and the negative can deliberately misconstrue, the King's words. It's easy to make a liar out of someone whom we wish to make a liar. Those who have no love nor respect for the King will make his text appear to be whatever they wish it to be. To see the King's text as it is, they must allow the King's Spirit to prepare them. One cannot judge a thing from outside of it, without judging it wanting. If they first condemn a perfectly just and wholly compassionate King, then rejecting his incomparable words follows easily enough. We can beg them, *listen, dear friends, to* the King's truths, but they won't listen. He would tell them things that their arrogance hides from them, but they simply won't listen.

We make no such error, my brother. An unprepared reader might shudder at the events of Abraham's near-sacrifice of his son Isaac. Here the King's Father seemed to tell Abraham to sacrifice Isaac on an altar and then to burn the Isaac's body in a fire. The unprepared reader might think it terrible that Abraham nearly carried out the act, gathering the wood for the fire, tying the child to the altar, and raising the knife to slay Isaac. Surely Abraham's act demonstrated incredible devotion to the Father's will, yet what should we think of a Father who would demand such a sacrifice? What should we think of a person who would offer it? Even though the King is the *rock whose works are perfect,* an unprepared reader might misunderstand the account of Abraham's near-sacrifice of Isaac.

Yet we read about this event, as we read any other event that the King's text describes, informed by the King's Spirit. Abraham lived in a time and place where the people worshiped gods to whom they sacrificed children. Abraham's Father, the one true living God, called a halt to Abraham's near-sacrifice of Isaac. *Don't lay a hand on that boy! Don't touch him!* The sacrifice did not occur. The Father stopped it. He did not ask again for the sacrifice of a child and never in any instance received it, whether before or after Abraham's near-sacrifice of Isaac. To the contrary, Abraham's Father, our Father, my dear brother, tries to *convince parents to look after their children,* while threatening to destroy any land where the parents refuse to do so. The King's heart is for children.

In our one great spiritual mystery, the Father later offered his own son the King as a sacrifice to bring all of us including the son back to him. Abraham's near-sacrifice of Isaac foreshadowed the Father's greatest act that at the same time gave the King his greatest glory. In the account of Abraham's near-sacrifice of Isaac, the Father stopped us from doing that which was to him repugnant, even though it was then and is today common to sacrifice children, while at the same time he did the same thing for us to demonstrate the extent of his own love for us and to bring us back to him. The lesson of Abraham's near-sacrifice of Isaac depends not only on seeing the historical context and the result among Abraham's people but also on seeing its connection to the nature, role, and purpose of the King as the Father's sacrificed Son. The story of Abraham's near-sacrifice of Isaac teaches us the opposite of that which an unprepared reader might think, that our Father is an unfathomably compassionate God who abhors our harming one another, especially our children. Because Abraham was willing to listen to the Father, the Father *made sure that our children flourish.*

Our generation, my brother, should be especially careful about condemning the ancients for sacrifice of children, or worse, condemning the Father for asking Abraham's near-sacrifice of Isaac. Don't people sacrifice their children today to many false gods? Don't they pursue lifestyles and pleasures, take risks, and engage in behaviors that threaten, harm, and destroy millions of their children? One must be blind to one's own sin and blind to the clarity of the King's teaching on parenting to condemn the Father and his Son the King as uncaring toward children. The King says, *Let the children alone, don't prevent them from coming to me*, adding that his kingdom is filled with them.

Where must we be, then, dear brother, to let the King speak lessons of life to us rather than draw from those rich lessons their opposite, which would be death and condemnation? They who reject the King and *refuse to obey the message will pay for what they've done*. And you know what? Their greatest punishment will be that they not get to see the King. We must prepare ourselves further, my brother, and let the King's Spirit prepare us further. The King's Spirit must work in us to soften our will and make supple our minds so that we can understand and will accept these teachings. We need the King's Spirit to *cut away the thick calluses on our hearts, freeing us to love him*. In our natural condition as it is, we do not always easily or readily appreciate what we should of him. We were *wrong before we were born*. We need his Spirit in us to appreciate him. It isn't exactly natural to get everything he tells us. Understanding of that kind is instead work of his Spirit. We can still discuss his words in meaningful ways, even though we seldom grasp them adequately in all dimensions. Reading the King's text productively depends on the presence and work of the King's Spirit.

How do we reach that place where we can read the King's text productively through the work of the King's Spirit? Spiritual influences are not so foreign a concept to the modern mind, my friend, even though we might think of ourselves in more material and less spiritual terms. Popular and psychological thinking acknowledge the positive and negative influences of different kinds of attitudes, thinking, and emotions, that together we might as well call spirit. Within organizations and sports, we readily accept the idea and influence of team spirit. Counselors address spirits of insecurity, anxiety, and depression. In marriages, we readily recognize the positive and negative influences of spirits of trust or suspicion.

Spiritual thinking is not so unusual for us. We do it all the time. We know that these spirits, or conditions of our way of thinking, influence our outlook, decisions, relationships, even our physical health. It makes perfect practical sense. The wise seldom fall victim to the wrong spirit. We know better. Instead, negativity finds *unsuspecting souls it can bedevil.* Once negativity sets in, it draws in other worse attitudes that gradually corrupt the whole person. They give one wrong spirit a toehold, and other wrong spirits join it, until the whole attitude is so bad that nothing works.

What we have discovered that not everyone understands, Memphis, is that the King's Spirit is distinct from other good spirits. It is not just about being positive and upbeat. That kind of simple spiritual thinking is just not enough to keep us right. We need something, or indeed someone, far stronger and complete. The King's Spirit is not merely the team spirit, marked by unity and camaraderie. Nor is the King's Spirit simply one of comfort and joy, although his Spirit includes those attributes. The King does not limit his Spirit to any constellation of attitudes or emotions. Instead, the King's Spirit has all of those attributes reflected in the complete life and teachings of the King. The King's Spirit is the whole King, not apart from and less than the King. The King's Spirit *reminds us of all the things* that the King's text tells us about the King. The King's Spirit is the King's presence, the revealer and teacher of the King's personified truth, constantly *confirming the truth, the reality of* the King's presence.

As we read the King's text, we need to be in that place where the King's Spirit informs us. We need not to be in the culture, or in the limits of our education, or held back by the views and attitudes of those around us. The King's Spirit guides us into the King's truth, not into an exercise of the human imagination. It is pretty simple, even if it seems mysterious. When the *Spirit of the Truth comes, he takes us by the hand and guides us into all the truth there is,* which is the King's truth. The Spirit makes sense out of what the King said and did. We must sort of tie ourselves to the Spirit like a lifeline, for the Spirit to pull us from that which distracts, depletes, and ultimately destroys us, toward that which gives us the King's priceless forever love. The Spirit's guides us so effectively and unerringly that we discover the path of genuine life. Even while we sleep, the Spirit shapes our willingness to accept the King's instruction. Reading the King's text with the Spirit's aid allows us to read for revelation, not in a spirit of doubt but in victory. It is pretty extraordinary, this Spirit thing.

I do not go too far to say that when they read the King's text without the King's Spirit, their reading does little or nothing for them. They do themselves little good reading the text dry, in bad humor, without the Spirit. When we read with the Spirit, the King *brings gifts into our lives much the same way that fruit appears in an orchard.* Without the Spirit, they are unlikely to draw any inspiration from it or produce any fruit. They do not change. They get nothing special said or done. They could even become scholars of the King's word and yet not produce the King's fruit. They might, as Paul writes, fathom all mysteries and all knowledge, and even have great faith showing wonderful gifts of prediction and insight. Yet if they do not show the Spirit's love for the King, they are nothing and gain nothing. They can even *make everything as plain as day* about the King, but if they do it without the King's sort of love, it does them and others nothing. Without the Spirit, they might simply put aside the King's text, failing to appreciate it enough to put it to the good use for which the King intended it. The Spirit must work in them as they read the King's text, for their reading to be effective.

You, though, my brave brother, know how to draw from the Spirit who makes reading the King's text worthwhile. We do so in part through thinking of the King, meditating on the King, even talking to the King. We put aside other things to celebrate the King. They do not receive the King's Spirit simply by calling for him like they would call a dog, even though calling could be a good place for them to start if they did it the right way. They need not, indeed they could not, call the King's Spirit down from heaven. Their broken condition leaves them no authority in that realm. What they need and what we have is the King himself. Only the King can give us the gift of his Spirit. They need to be *cleaned up and given a fresh start* just as the King cleaned us up and let us start over. Ever since the King left, we have had the King's Spirit among us as guide and counselor. We only need to accept the King himself to get the King's Spirit fully inside us. Yes, that's right, the Spirit *himself within us.*

It may seem odd, but it's not. The King's Spirit inhabits those of us whom the King prepares for the Spirit. You've seen people take on the likeness of almost anything, imitating you-name-it once it gets inside of them. The King's Spirit, though, only gets inside those whom the King cleans up. You won't see the Spirit in a mess. The Spirit inhabits us when we attend to the King's interests, meet the King's concerns. When we give up our will for the will of the King, then the Spirit gets comfortable with us. It would not make sense any other way, would it? You wouldn't expect a good soldier to take in a traitor, would you? Once in us, the King's Spirit does more work cleaning up our minds and softening our will for more of the King. We all need that cleaning up. *There's no one without it.* To ignore the Spirit's role in this process of preparing us for reading is to lose sight of what makes our reading work. We talk to the King, put things aside for the King, and prepare for the King's Spirit, so that we can read the King's text better and better. We then see and understand what we never before saw in the King's text, things that remain hidden from others.

We should also consider where reading the King's text takes us. Some misunderstand the destination, thinking that following the King's text means leaving home or workplace. The King's text actually says just about the opposite. It says to some of us to stay right where we are after we start reading his text and loving the King. We stay living in the same home with the same family and stay working for the same employer. Even while conducting his missionary journeys, Paul earned his way using his old skills as a tentmaker. He and others who taught about the King *worked together at their common trade*, just as we continue to work at our professions. Resolute reading of the King's text need not lead us away from relationships and skills and into isolation. Instead, our change occurs where we have the greatest need, inside of us. Our reading first makes us better off for ourselves and others, right where we are, with right what we are presently doing.

With our reading, though, we also find ourselves moving in different places. At first, our change may be only on the inside. Looking out from inside, we find the world brighter, more joyful, and less anxious. The world may actually be just as threatening. Yet our perspective changes as we get to know and begin to act on the King's words. We find a place within ourselves and within the King's Spirit now dwelling within us, of greater peace, purpose, and security. He *gets our feet on the life path,* giving us his confidence like he knows the outcome and that the outcome is good. What he makes for us inside seems to be our own special place, not something that everyone else has but just for us. Of course, that care makes perfect sense about one who made us in our mother's womb. Before he *shaped us in the womb, he knew all about us.* So he would know how to make us right inside.

We then find ourselves in new places we would never before have had the courage or reason to visit. We might never have visited places where people who do not even know us would give us a warm hug. We find places where people actually speak on our behalf, indeed speak to the King for us. Imagine that. We find places that transform us with each visit, where we soon participate in the transformation of others. We find ourselves healed there from old scars that we hardly knew we were carrying. He gradually makes of us a *great success*, when there didn't seem much hope for that success. We find friends we would never have known without the King, whom we can trust and on whom we can depend, just as they can trust and depend on us. We find ourselves speaking in those new places with new and unfamiliar purpose. We find ourselves singing even if never before a singer or playing musical instruments even if never before musicians. Reading the King's text can take us anywhere.

Reading the King's text also takes us to places of service. Those places transform our outlook as to others, my adventurous brother. We find in our business new opportunities to serve those who most need our service. Somehow, we never *show up empty handed* because that is exactly what the King commands. We always manage to offer just what we are capable of offering. In those places of service, we find new friends, even teachers, when our prior arrogance and insularity, before we knew the King, would have kept us from those friends and teachers. When we are weak and without help, the King's text takes us to places where we find strong people willing to share resources. When we are strong and with resources, the King's text leads us among those with whom we can share. When we do it the King's way, it *turns out well.*

Reading the King's text can take us anywhere. Consider the King's own figures. The exiled slave youth Daniel and the orphaned girl Esther each rose to power in foreign kingdoms ruled by their Jewish nation's adversaries. Neither could reasonably have aspired to those positions, but they both achieved them. It was the King. If either had announced such ambition and made their own efforts to bring it about, they would promptly and properly have been condemned as treasonous. Yet because their humility and faith was like that of the King and from the King, they achieved seemingly impossible things with ease and grace. They just *stayed calm, minded their own business, and did their own job*, but look where they ended up. The same thing happened for the young shepherd David, making him king over Israel.

The King's followers end up all over the world in the most unlikely of places. They never imagined the possibility of such exciting work in such exotic places until they joined the King's work. We do not miss the opportunity to let the King direct us each to our own place, the place for which he uniquely suited us. Instead, we listen, we read, we *let it fall like a gentle rain* until it soaks us, and we start growing. We read the King's text with confidence that it will take each of us to our place for the greatest good, even when we cannot yet see it. *God took us out of Egypt with his strong hand and long arm, terrible and great, with signs and miracle-wonders, and he brought us to this place, gave us this land flowing with milk and honey.*

The new resident somehow knew the purpose of his visit to the mountainous region to which the King's smile had transported him in an instant. He would find here the answer to whether his parents, who had departed the old earth many years earlier, were also now kingdom residents. The new resident knew that the King held the only path to the kingdom. None entered who did not know and embrace the King. Kingdoms come in many forms, yet they all exist but for one reason, which is to honor their king. To dwell forever in this glorious place, the new resident's parents must have acknowledged their need of the King while they still had that choice on the old earth. The new resident had not witnessed that acknowledgment.

The path led him deeper into the mountains. In his old condition, he would have groaned at the exertion that the rising way foretold. He would have doubted his ability to supply it. Now, he felt nothing but exhilaration with every step up the steep path deeper into the spectacular mountains. The path began up a deep valley. As the new resident walked briskly on and up, the valley grew shallower. Soon, the valley disappeared entirely, and he walked instead on ridges still heading up toward the highest of the many peaks. Although he saw nothing but mountains, the new resident felt the strong presence of the King beckoning him on and up.

Finally, the path disappeared entirely beneath his feet. The way now no longer rose sharply up. His stride slowed as he approached what seemed to be the highest point of the tallest peak. The new resident slowly scanned the horizon, seeing nothing but a vast field of brilliant peaks, all just a little lower than the great peak at the pinnacle of which he now stood. As he turned, his eyes met the eyes of the King who he now realized had walked up the peak behind him. The King for a moment looked as if to shed a tear but instead stepped forward reaching toward the new resident. No tear would fall in the kingdom. The new resident began to kneel in submission, but the King caught and embraced him.

The King's embrace instantly returned the new resident to the valley farm, where the new resident's wife and daughter greeted him warmly. The new resident had returned with his answer. He had expected sadness but in the kingdom could feel none, sensing instead the depth and breadth of the King's wisdom. He knew without knowing, understood without understanding, trusting completely in the King whose embrace still suffused him. All was good, even if it had been other than he once would have desired. The King had desired it, making it equally perfect and complete for the new resident.

6

How

His first sensation on regaining consciousness was of holding tightly to the pack holding his brother's letter. He lay on a bed of reeds in the shade of a small grove at the trailhead to the ancient ruins. The desert guide was gently coaxing him to let go of the pack, which he eventually did only on the guide's promise to leave it resting against his side. He then learned of his dramatic rescue, as the guide tended to the wound on the back of his head.

The guide had no intention of following him into the ancient ruins. The guide had warned him of the risk of robbery or worse in the unpatrolled ruins. The guide had intimated that those who had nearly done them in near the start of their trip may well be waiting here for a more fruitful ambush. Yet as foreboding as the ancient ruins had been, he would not abandon his adventure at the very point of its success. Instead, the guide had himself felt compelled to follow him into the ruins. The guide could not explain his compulsion, particularly because his full compensation for the trip was securely in his pocket. It should have made no difference to him if his charge did not return in the good health with which he began his foolish quest. Yet the guide simply could not resist whatever or whoever compelled him to follow his charge into the ruins — though at a safe distance.

That distance had indeed proven their salvation. The guide had heard the robbers' sounds luring his charge onward. He had expected what his charge had not. His timing had once again been impeccable. Three shots had been enough to gain him time and room to collect his charge for a hasty retreat with his charge's slight unconscious frame draped over his shoulder. He still did not understand how he had made the trailhead so quickly while so heavily laden. Yet here they were, somewhat safe and mostly sound, now that his charge had regained consciousness. Foresight would have called the rescue foolishness. Hindsight made it a miracle.

The event (or perhaps the blow on the head) crystallized things that the traveler had mulled throughout this last trip. Yes, he now knew that this trip was his last. His chasing after ruins had come to an end with a realization that he did not expect but that might have been obvious to another. All of these years, he had sought answers precisely where they were least likely to lie, among the ruins of civilizations that had not found them. He now saw clearly the wrongness of his path. He had not found answers. Moreover, he had subjected not only himself but others to the risks, even if not quite the full consequences, of his error. He had nearly led himself and others to death among the ruins.

He patted the pack holding his brother's letter. He did not know what role the letter had played spurring him to this conclusion. In fact, he thought the letter quite odd, although odd in just the sense that his brother was so. Yet beyond the letter, or more precisely within the letter, he was reading a text that he now believed held the clue not to the dead but to the living. He sensed himself turning toward that new life as if a door had opened to him that he had long kept shut. He resolved to finish the letter on the journey back. He would then discuss with his brother this sense of turning toward a door now open to new life.

He nodded to the guide, who had finished attending to his wound. The guide helped him to his feet. His balance was still poor, but he felt up to walking. He knew that they needed to put some distance behind them. The camels ahead would help. His mind began to turn toward the trip home, which he had arranged to take him through the ancient holy city he had not yet visited on any of his prior trips. What had once seemed unattractive—the living worshipping a living God—had a new allure that he could not quite grasp, except that he knew it had something to do with his no longer chasing the dead.

As to how to read the King's text, my good brother, is it too simple to say that we open it to its first page and begin? The King's text is so extraordinary and precious of a thing that we hold a sense of awe when beginning. The King *takes care of the hidden things but the revealed things are our business.* The text is so singular that we must address it. Its start does not disappoint. *First this: God created the Heavens and the Earth—all you see, all you don't see.* Yet start to finish the first time may not be the best approach for every reader. We are each a little different as readers. Different strokes for different folks. Some of us will persevere in reading, while others will not. Some of us show discipline in reading, while others do not. Some of us are inveterate readers, while others are not.

Disciplined inveterate readers like us, my brother, might as well begin at the first page because we will read straight through. Reading a certain number of pages each day gives us a good daily goal. We want to pursue the King, to tell him to *let us in on his plans.* Start to finish, a little each day, accomplishes that pursuit. Some versions of his text conveniently divide it into daily readings, helping us know where to start and stop. They even give the calendar dates so that we can complete the whole text within one or two years. Some of those versions start at the beginning and go straight through to the end. Others give us readings from the old part of the King's text and the new part each day. Still others offer a daily mix of old-part history, old-part writings from Psalms and Proverbs, and new-part teachings and events. I love that good mix. We need read only a little each day for the reading to remind us of the whole text. We *keep the fire burning continuously* so that it never goes out.

Yet strong readers like us, my brother, would read the whole King's text much more quickly than in one or two years. An average reader needs only 79 hours to read the whole text, which means less than 15 minutes each day to complete it in one year. A strong reader with the discipline to read just an hour or so each day (and we certainly read more, my dear brother) will complete the King's text in just two months. With a little more discipline, a keen reader can read the whole text in just one month without interfering with work and family life. Habitual readers can reread the King's text every two to three months while maintaining a full life and exploring other texts. What does the King expect but that we *follow the road he sets out for us?* Reading his text each day, we do what he asks and live a good life.

Of course, reading pace means nothing if we do not grasp the content. We often do better reading slowly to ponder the text's times, places, events, and figures. Our best approach may be to reflect at length on a single passage or phrase, or to read a single chapter repeatedly until it resonates. Think of the benefit, my brother, of memorizing Paul's love chapter in his first letter to the Corinthians. *Love never gives up, love cares for others, love doesn't strut.* That single chapter reminds us just how far we are from real love. We think love means one thing, but it teaches us that love means something much greater. We could find no more informative or lyrical text. We could mine it and mine it over and over. Its meanings are unending. It remains fresh years after we first read it. It keeps informing us whenever we return to it.

Still, as literate as we may think ourselves, my friend, we do not always read like the accomplished reader. Undisciplined readers ought to begin the King's text where they will not easily be put off. That goal makes the first book Genesis a good place to begin for its fast pace and familiar content. The first 20 chapters of the next book Exodus have the same sense of real-life action. Yet the rest of Exodus and the next three books Leviticus, Numbers, and Deuteronomy, could discourage an undisciplined reader. The good news of John is then a great place to jump, especially with the way that it reflects Genesis's beginning. *The Word was first, the Word present to God, God present to the Word.* John's Gospel, the fourth of the overlapping stories of the King's life, may be the best place to start for the one who always finds reading to be a chore. One has only to read to John's third chapter to reach the fundamental of the King's faith — our faith, the faith that gives everyone a fresh start. *Forget about what's happened; don't keep going over old history.*

Matthew is another good-news book with which to encourage an undisciplined reader, my dear brother, beginning as it does with the treasured account of the King's birth. It also quickly reaches the King's revolutionary teaching in the message he gave on the Mount. When he teaches things like, *You're blessed when you are the end of your rope*, we see how different his way of thinking is. The shortest good-news book Mark is another good place for the undisciplined reader to go. Mark describes the King's actions in ways sure to keep a reader's attention. Then again, the contemporary tenor of Luke's good news also makes for accessible reading. Each of good-news book within the King's text has its own quality to recommend it. Who would want to miss reading about the dead Lazarus living again or about the last meal with the King?

Other readers enjoy the Psalms for their emotional poetry or Ecclesiastes for its philosophical style. The Song of Songs enchants some readers while Job and Esther are other favorites of many readers. Some readers need a certain book or chapter to anchor the rest of the King's in place or as a window through which to view the rest of the King's text. Among the prophetical books, readers often think of Isaiah as the window or anchor. Written centuries before the King came, Isaiah so clearly foreshadows his coming, and its call for servant-like justice is so relevant, that the book seems at once ancient and heraldic on one hand, and yet thoroughly modern on the other hand. Even in its histories, the King's text hides many treasures, like when Samson's father encountered the King's representative. Manoah asked him his name, but he answered, *You wouldn't understand — it's sheer wonder.* What of the classic stories of David and Goliath, and Daniel in the lion's den, or the visions in Ezekiel? What reader would want to miss Revelation's symbol-rich vision of the future?

Do you, though, my brother, know a reader less disposed to imagery or story and more interested in prosaic advice? The King's text has plenty of prosaic instruction, saying things like *be very careful to act exactly as* the King commands. We should share Proverbs with that reader who appreciates straight talk. Nothing is as direct and practical as Solomon's wisdom collection. For consistently rich explanation of all things important in the King's text, one can hardly do better than the letters of Paul beginning with Romans. To see the ups and downs of life explained the way they should be, and to be able to share those contours with others, we need only read Paul's letters. After all, Paul drew his lessons from a dramatic, life-changing encounter with the King and from pursuing the King's work after that encounter. Do you miss that wise uncle? We have him in Paul.

We, though, the strong readers that we are, do not hesitate to read and explore all books within the King's text, my friend. If reading in one area, whether histories, writings, prophecy, good news, or letters, seems unproductive at the moment, then we start in another place, until the discernment of the King's Spirit informs us sufficiently to appreciate all parts and the whole of the King's text. We begin to see the difference between the King's way and other ways. That distinction is so important that we need to share it with our friends. *"This is a lasting ordinance for the generations to come, so that you can distinguish between the holy and the common, between the unclean and the clean, and so you can teach the Israelites all the decrees the Lord has given them through Moses."*

We ought to consider also what we do while we read. Some readers highlight or underline those portions of the King's text that reach their conscience. Those readers can then more quickly locate the highlighted text, or when reading a second time, can recall that text as having been particularly meaningful. Some readers highlight in one color one time through and in another color another time through, to learn how their needs and interests change over time. Some highlight in one color for the attributes of the King and another color for his instructions. We have many ways to engage the King's text more actively than to just let it pass before our eyes. We just need to feel that thirst. *Hey there, all who are thirsty, come to the water!* The King's text has no cost.

Margin notes serve similar purposes. When we attend meetings, lessons, or studies of the King's text exploring certain parts, we make margin notes including date and speaker. Doing so helps us recall and connect key teachings to the particular text from which the speaker drew them. The King's text is the source of sound instruction. The more active we are as readers, brother Memphis, the better we understand and retain the text's meaning. Noting and grouping similar verses on note pages at the text's beginning and end can build a reference for us on various themes and issues. We can record citations to events, characters, or concepts to help with issues like addiction, depression, conflict, stress, and other topics. Making notes in the front and back of the text reassures us that we can quickly locate those key parts on which we most often and most surely rely. We do so rely because the King is *bedrock under our feet.* Jotting down in the front or back of the text names of those who ask for help, or matters about which we need instruction, personalizes the text. It helps us connect the King's text with important things going on in our lives and the lives of those for whom we most care.

Then, we might also keep separate journal of our reading. Occasionally writing down our thoughts about a certain passage can solidify its teaching. Another way to write reflectively about the King's text is to do so in letters to acquaintances, even as here, my dear brother. This way, we inform ourselves as much as we inform others. Indeed, I do not purport to instruct you or anyone but instead simply to encourage myself while hoping to do likewise in some small measure for you and others. Writing about the King's text serves both reader and writer. When we find the right readers, we receive back their own letters and insights. Saving those letters lets us see how our understanding has grown, how we resist the King's Spirit less and less. *Don't go against him. He won't put up with our rebellions.*

The order of our reading is only one set of clues to effective reading of the King's text, my dearest friend. How we interpret the text's events offers another set of clues for drawing more of what the text offers us. We benefit by thinking of the King's text not only as history but as allegory. The text clearly works as both. The King's events actually occurred, and thus we should read the text in that historical manner. Only by doing so can we fully appreciate the wonder of the King's work. Yet to read the King's text solely as history would be to miss its work in our lives today, that is, miss its lessons as allegory. We should read about the King's figures and events not only as history but as patterns for what we exhibit, encounter, and experience today. The King's events can represent circumstances that we face today. The attitudes and actions of the King's figures can represent attitudes we reflect and actions we take today. His lessons mean that much to us because he *found us out in the wilderness, in an empty, windswept wasteland, and then threw his arms around us and lavished attention on us.*

You know the following example, my dear brother, as a pattern for our own miraculous escapes from our own figurative prisons. Luke describes in Acts Peter's release from prison. Peter slept until the King's representative appeared. Light shone in Peter's prison cell, the representative struck Peter to wake him, and Peter's chains fell off. The representative clothed Peter to escort him out of prison past the guards with the last gate swinging open on its own. As a historical matter, we must accept that the miracle of Peter's freedom occurred. Peter was surely imprisoned but just as surely escaped to continue the King's work. This ancient event, though, means much to us today if we also treat it as allegory. Do not we also sleep in figurative prisons? Sometimes, it is obvious to others how asleep we are when we hardly see it ourselves. The wrongs of *some people are blatant and march them right into court.* But then, the right perspective arrives and we correct what we are doing when the King's representative is present. The King sometimes just has to strike us to wake us up and get our attention. Our chains then fall off. The King escorts us out of our figurative prisons, our enemies hardly recognizing us. These miracles occur not by our effort but by the King's good will and work. Those who fail to read the King's text as allegory miss its life-changing lessons.

Another example you know well, my brother, is the story of the queen of Sheba's visit to Solomon. That visit fascinates as a historical account, coming as it does at the height of the material riches of the nation of Israel. Yet the lesson for us today could be just as fascinating and more meaningful. Reading it closely, we recall that the queen first tested Solomon—that which anyone who does not know the King might do, even today, when facing spiritual richness. People do test us, don't they? In Sheba's case, *she came to put his reputation to the test by asking tough questions.* Only after Solomon passed her test did the queen share with Solomon what she really had on her mind. That's the way it usually works. As soon as someone sees that we know that about which we speak, then they open up. People are always confessing their confusion to those who know the King and are not confused. That's the way we want it. The spiritually uninformed pour confusion and dissatisfaction from their hearts, right after their initial hard testing of us.

Solomon's response was just as important, my friend. He did not leave her hanging. He answered the queen's hard questions. She *talked to him about all the things she cared about, emptying her heart to him.* And Solomon gave it to her straight, leaving nothing unanswered. We are just as willing to respond effectively when someone opens their confused heart to us, which is really to say, to the King because all we do is represent the King. Solomon's wisdom overwhelmed the queen, the King's text tells us, which remains the King's effect today when we share his wisdom. The queen's next response was to confess that although she had heard of Solomon's wisdom, she had not believed it. Confession remains the genuine response today of those who first read the King's text including Solomon's wisdom and accept it for what it is. They see how profound it is. Solomon's final response was to give the queen more gifts than she had brought him, which is equally the result today when a reader encounters the King's text. They do not leave empty handed. The reader receives more than the reader gives. The King's text offers so much more when we see its events as allegory for our lives today.

The King's text also operates powerfully on a broader level, as you well know, my dear friend. For example, we appreciate Genesis's story of Noah after the flood for its simple beauty. When the rains ended, Noah first released a raven, which returned to the ark after flying back and forth across the waters. He then released a dove, which on the first release returned but on the second release brought back an olive leaf and on the third release remained away. *Noah knew that the flood was about finished.* In this manner, so touching in its simple account, Noah confirmed that the floodwaters had receded. The dove had found a resting place where an olive tree could grow. That conclusion might be all that some readers would draw from the story, beautiful but without any other particular meaning.

Yet when we read the account of Noah in a broad figurative sense, we know that it foreshadows the spiritual ages of the earth. To some readers, the raven that Noah released to fly back and forth across the floodwaters represents the devil sewing evil across the face of the old earth. The dove represents the King's Spirit whose first flight represents the old age, second flight (with olive leaf) the age of the King, and third flight our age when the King's Spirit remains with us while we await the return of the King. We resist the flood by building on the King's rock. The King's text supplies *foundation words, words to build a life on.* When we build on his words, we have strong and stable lives. When we do not build on his words but build on anything else, our lives are wrecks waiting to happen, disasters in the making.

The King's text makes that much difference. The King's text is not simply history but also allegory containing figures, themes, patterns, and types. Swords in the King's text may represent the King's incisive words, water in the King's text may represent the source of life, a rock may represent the King himself as a foundation for life, a lamp or light may represent truth, and so on. We ought to read remembering that the King's text uses names, places, animals, and events to represent larger and deeper meanings.

Yes, Memphis, reading for effect has more to it than tracing the words across the page. As we read about the King's figures and their actions, we ask ourselves to whom the figures listen, whether the King or man. For example, Ahaziah, injured by accident, doubted his recovery, just as we suffer emotional wounds when others hurt us by accident, and just as we doubt our own recovery. Ahaziah made the fatal mistake of consulting not the King but charlatans who were out to kill him. Charlatans may tell blind leaders what they want to hear, but their counsel will be those leaders' destruction. Those who listen to the counsel of others who do not have the listeners' best interests at heart will not prosper. The prophet Elijah told Ahaziah that he would indeed die for having rejected the living King to receive deadly counsel. Ahaziah would *never get out of that bed alive*, once he had made his bed with those who reject and despise the King. We keep looking for the message in these events. The King's text does not record them simply to relate history. It records them to supply us with lessons, when we imagine ourselves in the same situations.

The text's description of the same event relates another lesson beyond the key lesson to listen only to the King and his counselors. Ahaziah died only after sending out three captains with their battalions to murder the prophet Elijah. Ahaziah did not merely reject the King's counselor Elijah. He wanted to destroy truth-telling, to have power win out over truth. The first two captains followed orders from Ahaziah to try to kill Elijah. Yet the King brought fire down from heaven to destroy those two captains. When they do the work of those who do not pursue the King's counsel, they too end up destroyed. The King does not insulate persons from consequences when they allow others to make decisions for them.

Following orders is not enough when those orders are to oppose the King. Ahaziah's third captain instead took the right action. Instead of trying to murder Elijah as Ahaziah had ordered, he acknowledged to Elijah the King's power. We too should acknowledge the King's power while rejecting the authority of anything else. The third captain asked Elijah's help in his predicament over having to carry out Ahaziah's order, saying, *O Holy Man, have respect for my life.* We too should ask for the counsel of the righteous, especially when it might look to us like we are about to oppose them. Elijah showed the third captain the King's mercy, sparing the captain and his men while also solving their predicament.

We also find different perspectives for reading the old and new parts of the King's text. We read the old part as the story of the old promise between God and his chosen people Israel. The old part portrays a people under God's law before the King brought the current age of grace. Heroes of the old part are not only flawed, like David in his adultery with Bathsheba, his conspiring to murder Bathsheba's husband, and his unwillingness to discipline his rapist son Amnon and treasonous son Absalom. Heroes of the old part are also without the King. Figures from the text's old part lack the King's model. We should not feel superior to them, though, because it *wasn't so long ago that we ourselves were stupid and stubborn.* Before we learned about and followed the King, we were haters who just pursued our own wants. The old promise introduced rather than completed the great plan.

Old-part books within the King's text, like Job, often contain more questions than answers. Job himself lamented, *How can mere mortals get right with God?* Job's lament is the quandary in which old-part figures find themselves without the King's saving grace. Job knew this quandary, pleading for the King's help, *How I wish we had an arbitrator to step in and let me get on with life.* Now that we have perfect hindsight since the King's coming, we cannot mistake Job's lament over man's condemned condition before the King for our present joy and freedom in the King. We instead remember the old part's role foreshadowing the King. That recollection helps us recognize the old part's limitation, that it is only the first part of the King's great advent. The old part begins the plan rather than completes it. It foreshadows the King's coming as a way to mediate between us and the father so that we can come to agreement and get together once again. We do not mistake old-part books like Job and Ecclesiastes as answers when they are instead questions. They pose the question to which the new part gives the answer in the King's coming. Misreading the old part, we might conclude that we lead innocent but hard lives under God's difficult rules. Instead, old-part rules reflect God's perfection while proving us imperfect and needing the King.

We read the new part of the King's text differently, my friend. The new part reveals the King and his Father as loving and forgiving, showing how the King saves us from the old rules. The new part confirms that we remain as twisted and corrupted as we have been since Adam promptly disobeyed the first and only rule. Yet the new part also shows that the King freed us from our corruption and the associated violation of rules. Here finally is a *word we can take to heart and depend on,* that the King made the final difference in getting us set right again. The old promise is obsolete, though still important in explaining the King's role. We no longer live always breaking rules, sure of our final destruction. We instead join the King following his rich way of life, so rich in love, joy, and peace that we can find no better. We know that *one day spent in his house beats thousands* of days in the best place on earth.

Yes, my dear friend, we read the King's text with love for the King. We feel passionate about that love, like we have nothing more important. If anyone wants to know the full truth, then let's tell them. We are *madly in love with him.* We do not ignore the old part of the King's text. It is important to getting the message of the whole thing, while it has its own fascinating history and teachings. Yet we keep the whole text in its proper context and perspective that it is all about the King. Face it: we were nothing. Then came the King, who *did it out of sheer love for us.*

The new resident had one last question that he knew the King would answer, although he knew not how or when the King would answer it. The new resident had a brother who had outlived him on the old earth, even though the brother was the older. Would that brother be joining them in the King's paradise, as the new resident had long desired? The days passed joyfully for the new resident in the valley farm, even as the question of his brother's destiny remained. The new resident frequently thought of asking the King but knew that the King had anticipated and fully knew the new resident's question without him needing to ask it. The kingdom held every desire of the heart.

The new resident stood on a hill overlooking the valley farm when he sensed the great presence beside him. The King looked deep into the new resident's eyes. His look conveyed a challenge that the new resident had not expected. The King's angel would show the new resident a glimpse of his brother's present journey. The challenge would have confused and concerned the new resident if he had not drawn such strength and solace from the King's gaze. His brother's fate the King had apparently not yet decided. That fate was still in the hands of his brother, even though the King certainly knew his brother's heart and its eternal result. The new resident had only to trust the King, which he did completely.

The new resident needed the King's strength for the visit. The new resident descended to the old earth holding fast to the wings of the King's great angel. The sky darkened with every descent. Together, angel and resident plunged through an atmosphere thick with choking smoke from sulfurous fires of heavenly battle. The angel's twisting flight just managed to avoid the weapons of legions of demons intent on preventing their descent. Other angels fought in pitted battle to distract the demons from their defense of the old earth. The prayers of earthly saints rose like shining lights to strengthen the angels in their awful battle, which the resident now knew was for his brother's soul.

They broke through into sunlight nearer the old earth's surface. The angel directed the resident's attention to the ruins of Egypt, where the resident now saw his brother kneeling and weeping beside a dead guide. His brother took no notice of armed bandits approaching nearby. The resident looked anxiously at the angel whose transfixed gaze remained on the brother. The resident felt the angel tense underneath him, the resident gripping the angel's wings harder in instinctive anticipation. Just then, his brother looked up into an empty sky, his lips moving even as he wept over the dead guide. His brother's prayer ignited and released the angel, who instantly swooped the last 100 feet to the brother just as one of the bandits raised a weapon to the back of the brother's head. The angel caught up the brother an instant before the weapon discharged.

The next moment, the angel was laying his brother in a Jerusalem hospital bed. The angel and resident stood invisibly by the brother's bed side as medical attendants worked. When the attendants had left, the angel pulled from its raiment the resident's long bundled letter, placing it on the sleeping brother's chest. The action awoke the brother whose hands grasped the letter in wonder. The brother slowly untied the strings to open the letter. He flipped the ragged pages over to a marker where he then began to read. The angel looked at the resident who slowly but dutifully resumed his place aboard the angel's back for the return flight. The resident wanted to speak to his brother, but the angel's look had instantly silenced him. The letter must suffice.

7

Why

He turned over the last page of the letter, reached for the string by the hospital bedside, and tied it neatly around the worn package. Curious indeed, he thought, but so like his brother. He looked forward to seeing his brother again, even while he wondered why his brother had not returned his calls. He was always the first to welcome him back from one of his adventures. This adventure had been the most unusual of them all, giving him much to discuss with his brother. He thought again of his brother's poor condition when he had last seen him but then put the thought quickly out of mind.

He recalled the guide's explanation of his rescue from the ancient ruins but could not recall how he had gotten from the guide's care outside the desert ruins to this hospital in Jerusalem. He had only a dream of the guide dying by gunshot and then of a great angel guided by his brother having brought him to the hospital. The physicians and attendants had only smiled knowingly when he related his dream. Many patients, they said, reported similar dreams of reaching this hospital. Yet they knew nothing specific of his coming, only that he had arrived in very poor condition but was healing enough to leave soon. He had long ago planned his return by air through Jerusalem. Those who had rescued him following his injury in the ruins must have discovered his itinerary and brought him here. Perhaps someday he would know. That was all that they could say.

The day of his discharge soon came. He thanked the hospital staff warmly before stepping curbside into the airport cab. Halfway to the airport, he realized that he had left his brother's letter on the bedside stand at the hospital. He ordered the cabbie to return to the hospital where the cab had picked him up, but the cabbie only gave him a curious look. No, he insisted, they must return to the hospital where the cab had picked him up. The cabbie shrugged and dutifully turned the cab around at his direction, retracing their route. Yet when they reached the block where the hospital had stood, he saw nothing but low dusty huts. He ordered the cab to a stop in the middle of the block where the hospital had stood. They sat silently in the cab for a few minutes.

Finally, he motioned to the cabbie, repeating the brief instruction that he had given when he first entered the cab, to head to the airport. Halfway there, the cabbie engaged his strange rider in the usual banter, learning that he had not yet explored the holy city. Did he not wish to do so? Great prophets had died there, he added, including the one whom they called the incarnate God. Something in the cabbie's tone made his rider think beyond the light banter. He noticed the cross swinging from the cab's rearview mirror. Yes, he indicated, he would indeed like to explore the holy city, if the cabbie might help him do so. The airport could wait. He might not be back this way again.

Finally, my brother, we reach the question of why we read the King's text. What is our purpose in reading? My letter about who, what, when, where, and how of reading the King's text has already suggested several reasons for reading. Yet we still have a last few things to consider. The text itself has important things to say about why we should know and share the King's words. Those who, like Paul, recorded the King's text tell us that they are *on our side, right alongside us.* They want us to have the full love of the King poured right into us, which is what happens when we read his text properly. Love pours right in, along with truth and discernment. We can see things in ourselves and others that we used not to see. We read the text to know the King, then sharing forever in his incomparable riches. We read *brimming with knowing God-Alive,* a living sort of knowledge that helps us love like the King.

Think with me about what that purpose means to us. The King's text is unlike any other book. Its poetry and prose have unique aesthetic qualities. The figures it describes formed and led a unique people with a unique purpose. The events that it describes comprise a unique perspective on history and society that continues to play itself out. The King's text had dozens of authors, recorders, really, contributing to it over more than a millennium. No other writing approaches such a continuous composition. The King's text includes the oldest writing we will ever read. Nothing else readily available to us comes close to its antiquity. The King's text records events in such poignant detail as to make us weep. We read specifics of lives, like Job's, lived millennia ago. Across millennia, Job tells us, *When I walked downtown and sat with my friends in the public square, young and old greeted me with respect.* He adds that people knew him for helping others, that he cheered the bereaved and stopped thieves. The King's text mixes with such detail, epic poetry, prose, and song of nation's victory over nation, all reflected through great figures' lives.

Yet a far greater distinction for both of us, my dear brother, is that the King's text is at the same time a thoroughly spiritual work. Its great subject is the wholly numinous incarnate God. Event after event make his majesty clear. Even something so worldly as Joshua's military conquest of Jericho he makes an inexplicable work of the divine. Joshua does not simply attack. He first encounters the commander of the army of the King. *He looked up and saw right in front of him a man standing, holding his drawn sword,* before whom Joshua must fall to his face in reverence. That figure, the King's commander who appears and disappears without trace, reminds Joshua that the victory is the King's victory, the only right side the King's side. With the King, we lose nothing. Without him, we win nothing.

The text's other-worldliness is unmistakable. We have only to read the Jewish historian Josephus's description of the same events and people over the same period, written around the same time as the new part of the King's text, to see how different and richer the King's text is than any merely historical writing. Josephus's historical writing even draws on the same sources as the recorders of the King's text. Yet reading Josephus is like reading a schoolbook compared to the mysterious other-worldliness of the King's text. We read the King's text because of it is completely different, events and meanings that we find nowhere else.

The text's fundamental difference from all other writings may not alone convince us to read it. We admit, my dear brother, that other writings are also different in other respects. Authors write without punctuation, just to be different. They write without narrative, just to be different. They write of things completely imagined, just to be different. Yet reading the King's text for the uncanny qualities of the King accomplishes something that reading other unique books does not. The King's text feeds that space within us. We are space-inside beings who require some sort of space-inside sustenance. Not everyone feeds this inside space. If they neglected their bodies the way that they neglect their inside space, then they would have died long ago. They constantly feed their minds, spending so much time and money on doing so that whole industries entertain it. Reading the King's text simply attends to that third part of our own nature in body, mind, and what we could call spirit. We read the King's text to survive and prosper in that inside-space spirit. *You gave bread from heaven for their hunger, you sent water from the rock for their thirst.*

To say that the King's text feeds the spirit, though, is to soften for the ear something that the text itself says more directly about our need for the King's food. When the King taught in person, his hearers may have required far less convincing than people do today to accept their need for spiritual transformation. The ancients may have had a clearer sense of how far they had fallen, down to the violence of the real Sodom and Gomorrah. The *cries of the victims of Sodom and Gomorrah were deafening,* so much so that they brought down the King. The figures of the King's text recognized their needful condition, that depravity was natural and abounded, far more readily than do people today.

Do we even use the word depravity, or is that just too judgmental? The King could then speak directly to the hearer's knowledge that the hearer needed new spirit, the King's Spirit. Today, the King's text must first overcome the sense that everyone is okay and that anything goes. They believe incorrectly that they have no deep-rooted or fundamental flaw. Oh, but the King will convince them otherwise, his text saying that he *will break their strong pride.*

Failing to see one's own flaws is not solely their problem, Memphis, but a problem that we share with others. We better think about ourselves in this area first. We need to follow the

King respectfully enough that it feels like fear, and then follow *him honestly and heartily.* If we do not do so, then we too will die apart from him and desperate. Here's how we can tell our need for getting better at following him. Imagine others could hear our thoughts, that every idle word that popped up in our consciousness during the course of one day were broadcast aloud to those around us without our being able to filter what others heard. We would probably find ourselves at the end of the day thoroughly embarrassed, maybe even unemployed and without friend. The petty jealousies, trivial sneers, and snide judgments that our poor minds so readily generate would, if exposed, ruin us.

No possibility of meaningful society would exist unless we were (as we are) able to conceal and correct our thoughts before we express them. But remember, we conceal nothing from the King. He knows our first thought and last. And we should want it no other way. We want him to *cross-examine and test us, get a clear picture of what we are about,* and then show it to us. That last part is how the King's Spirit works, showing us ourselves as we really are, which is as we appear to the King. We don't need to know so much how we appear to others. They pretty much tell us so. We can read them, although sometimes we can fool them. We can never fool the King. What matters to us is how the King sees us because he sees us exactly as we are, through and through.

Next, imagine that a camera recorded everything to which we directed our eyes during the course of a day, and that the record then played back for all to see. Again, what we had allowed to tempt, occupy, and distract us would humiliate us. Some days, we hardly look with love at those most precious to us but linger long over the most useless of things, whether in various writings, pictures, video, or the settings and movements around us. We should know how bad our distraction looks like to the King. See, they *die in their unclean condition,* those who do not have the King to clean them up.

We see in the face of such records, dear friend, that only hypocrisy or humility permit our survival. The King rightly saved his greatest condemnation for the hypocrite, particularly the religious hypocrite. He knew that the obviously corrupt, meaning the prostitute or drunkard whose faults are evident to all of us, have no privilege of hypocrisy. But then, because hypocrisy is unavailable to them, they have greater opportunity over the hypocrite for getting clean by following the King. Others whose corruption is less obvious but there nonetheless, hide their corruption behind their relative wealth, standing, education, and other advantages. Yet they face the greater obstacle to reaching out to the King exactly because they can hide their faults.

Few see the full depth of their faults. They fool themselves into believing that they have fewer of them and that the faults that they have are not so deep. The problem is that when they succeed in fooling themselves, then in their blind pride their faults become deeper than ever. They gradually become worse and worse, *self-absorbed, money-hungry, self-promoting, stuck-up, and profane.* They may look good, at least on the outside. That's the hypocrisy thing. But we know enough to steer clear of them. *Run for your life from all this* mess, my wise friend, and instead pursue the King. For me, I am almost more comfortable around those who cannot hide what they do or what they think. They just have one fewer obstacle to overcome than the hypocrites do.

We need not be scholars to lead the right kind of King-pursuing lives, dear brother. While scholars may know Hebraic and Aramaic texts, and that knowledge can help, we can still read reliable translations. The twelve men whom the King chose first to follow him were uneducated laborers. Yet after having followed the King, they acquired extraordinary wisdom, the ability to make others better instantly, and the courage to speak out about the King when it would cost them the most. *Upstart apostles were instructing the people* whom the religious experts used to instruct. Of course, their instruction upset the experts, even though the experts immediately recognized both the extraordinary quality of their teaching and the courage they showed in sharing it. The experts also knew that the King was the upstarts' source. Likewise, the King, not expert knowledge, is the source of our own wisdom and instruction. We can show too much pride in reading the King's text or our text knowledge, just as we can of other pursuits and accomplishments. We should remember that the insight is the King's, not ours. Without that humility, we cannot call ourselves the King's students or teachers. Even the King attributed his message to the *message of the Father who sent him.*

While we should not claim expertise in reading the King's text, we still embrace that reading the King's text and knowing his words bring us closer to the King. That is certainly how we learn his teaching. The King himself repeatedly relied on and referred to the old part of the text. He even said that it *takes a steady stream of words* from the text to stay alive. Natural food is not enough for life. When our one great enemy challenged him directly, the King quoted the old part of the text to serve the Father with *absolute single-heartedness.* The King also chastised his hearers who did not know the old parts of the text, saying they were *way off base, and here's why,* that they did not know the text's old parts such as the experiences of Moses, who learned from the burning bush that the King's Father was the Father of the living rather than the dead. Religious experts make religion too much about the dead, when to the King, it's the living who matter.

We have yet more profound reason to read, my friend. The King's text holds that its words are simply truth—not true but truth. What a difference the truth makes. Those who do not know truth but know that we have that truth *hate us because of it.* It is that powerful, that distinctive. The King's words remove us from the world's ways even as we remain here moving through the world like everyone else. We just move in a different direction, the King's direction. Others can tell that we are swimming in a different stream, a powerful stream that gives us special life. They see it in us. We succeed in our endeavors because we know and speak the King's truth. The King embodies truth, becomes truth. He even said, *I am the road, also the truth, also the life.* Truth has no standard beyond the King's words. We cannot measure accuracy, insight, or moral and spiritual content by anything higher than the Creator's words. That we know truth by the King's words ought to be sufficient reason to read them.

Truth defeats assault from which you and I are not immune, my only brother Memphis. The King's word does not only inform but also defends and protects us. We should *take all the help we can get* from the King's word because the battles we face are many, even daily. We may not fight hand to hand, but we sure fight in so many other ways that affect us and those around us deeply. It is as if we are under constant attack, and again, not so much bodily but in keeping a good attitude while we see and deal with everything coming our way.

I am not being abstract or overly spiritual when I write of truth, my brother. Even popular culture recognizes truth, albeit of a different character. They mistake truth to mean conditions or events confirmed by witnesses. Yet piling up facts makes no difference in the things that are important. Facts are facts. We all have a lot of them. Instead, the kind of truth that protects and defends us is the way that we see our origin, nature, responsibility, opportunity, and condition. When we are grasping the King's truth, we are *developing a rule solid and dependable* that let's no harm stick to us. You've heard of Teflon reputations? The King's truth is that kind of protection that no one and nothing can drag us down by sticking to us. The King's truth just tosses those things away from us. So we find in the King's words the truth that really means something. We don't find it in some record made of our senses. When we have his words, the King is *right there with us, fighting with us against our enemies.*

Others miss the protective purpose to reading the King's text, in favor of pursuing their imaginations. The King is *here, ready to be found by those who haven't bothered to look*, and instead they let their imaginations lead them to the worst places. Saul consulted a medium to call up the dead in séance. All it did was push him to the point of suicide. The King holds out his hands to us, calls our names, and shows himself to us. He wants even those who do not go after him to find him. He *made himself available to those who haven't bothered to ask.* He just keeps calling, *I'm here, right here.* He calls us not out of mystical mountaintop experience, candle, or crystal but out of his text's perfectly understandable words. That is why we are *gentle listeners and teachers who keep cool,* so that people who do not know the King will get a grip on it and free themselves.

Isn't that the point? When we read the King's text, my dear one, we help not only ourselves but also those around us. As inveterate readers like us soon learn, our reading is not always for us but so that we have words for others. We counsel one another constantly, whether we realize it or not. Our words influence those around us, whether we admit it or not. During Josiah's reign, the high priest Hilkiah found in the temple the Book of the Law, lost for several hundred years. When he learned of the discovery, Josiah asked Hilkiah to inquire of our King what was in the book. Josiah knew that the King's words would determine his own condition and his nation's condition. When Josiah heard those words and embraced them, the result was the whole kingdom's renewal. In the King's text, we find reliable counsel with which to influence others. Even when they leave him, when they *come back, he welcomes them with open arms.*

We value the King's text as the source of counsel to help others, especially when we employ the text with thoughtful reflection and discernment. We can help others make relatively quick and lasting change for the better when we encourage them to follow the King's counsel. The key is to seek the King *while he's here to be found.* It does not really matter how far away they gone from him. The King's text helps us discern and replace subtle distractions with commanding attention to him. Although some might believe otherwise, instruction in the King's text is rarely if ever abstract. It always has its application. It is not nearly as abstract as modern therapies, for instance. The King instructs in exceedingly direct fashion, much more direct than we are used to hearing from others. That direct counsel often pairs advice on what not to do with advice on the opposite action one should do. It gets us coming and going.

We know this counsel, my brother, because we know the King's words. We long ago stopped judging others, replacing judgment of others with self-examination. We put off stubbornness in our ways and replaced it with submission to the King's ways. We replaced irritation with patience and love. We replaced gossip destroying others with words of encouragement. Trust long ago took the place of worry. Confidence took the place of doubt. For every wrong attitude, the King's text gave us a corresponding right attitude. *Our job is simply to speak out on the things that make solid doctrine.* Our task of change can be as direct as listening to ourselves talk aloud to another and listening to our inner voice, while altering that voice to conform to the King's way of having us talk.

In these small and large ways, the King's text helps us distinguish bad habits from good practices, leading us to the things we ought to do for ourselves and one another. It helps us reduce the bad and increase the good, right where we always have room to improve. In some ways, it may have been *best that we were lost for a while,* so that we could return free of those bad habits. We continue to pursue the King while telling others how much he has helped us, which is much better than to ignore him and go on in our bad old ways. We get to make the choice, bound by our faults or freed of them. The difference is that consequential because as the King said, his *truth will free us.* We pursue him and follow his text so that he can set us free. Funny, isn't it, that being slave to the King is the only way for us to be free? But then, it makes such good sense because the King has authority over everything, especially our faults.

My brother, we experience this change while reading the King's text. We might take a few days or couple of weeks to read Jeremiah's prophecy, one of the longer parts of the King's text. It isn't easy. Reading Jeremiah is like a real encounter. The King challenged Jeremiah with whether he had understood the King correctly, only afterward affirming Jeremiah, *Good eyes, I'm sticking with you*, that Jeremiah had understood. Reading Jeremiah helps us see the King's concern over our actions and the consequences of following or not following his instruction. Through his text, the King shows us his expectations, affirming the good plans he has for us, *plans to give us the future for which we hope*. At the same time, he warns us that he watches and waits for us to follow him because it is only by doing so that he can give us that future.

Reading Jeremiah, we learn to avoid laziness because time runs out. See, it is fine for us to have those hopes for a special future. We must act with urgency. The King wants it that way. His text reminds us that the *noble make noble plans, and stand for what is noble*. We should have those hopes and, beyond hope, make firm plans for the best. Following the King, we find ourselves with the means and opportunity to make good plans, and not just good for ourselves, but good for everyone. Plan something special, and then watch it come about. Just make it the sort of thing that the King would have us do. We have only the King with whom to really build. We have *only one foundation, the one already laid*, and that foundation is the King. We cannot build for ourselves in secret. If we build anything without the King's support, then the fire of his passion burns it down.

We draw those Kingly plans from reading the King's text, especially when we find ourselves without purpose. We do sometimes get tired of errands. That is when we look for the King's way, for the vitality and energy that go with it. When we wonder which way to turn in what sometimes seems like a trackless wasteland, the King's text shows us his path. He *does exactly what he promises — every detail* of it. He shows us the options to follow him or follow others. We then choose him, knowing that choices make differences. We follow not some harebrained scheme of our own but sure ways down which he has led others for generations. I do not want to end up down my own dead-end road. He even lets us ask of him *just one more thing — bless our families*, not just us, but our loved ones, too.

Jeremiah conveys the King's warning not to trust in deceptive words that are worthless, as many do. Those who do not follow the King do *just what they want to do, indulging any and every evil whim and getting worse day by day.* It just does not work for them. They find no one to whom they can turn for help. *Friend against friend, they've trained their tongues to tell lies.* And because they are so used to telling one another lies, they no longer can even see the truth. That inability to see truth is exactly why they reject the King. They no longer see that he speaks truth and stands for truth, indeed that he embodies truth. Jeremiah warns us not to compete with them in their meaningless pursuits. They will wear themselves out just in time to encounter real difficulty.

The King's text instead offers comprehensive, profound, and consistent teaching to any who will listen. Its concepts reconfigure our thinking into thoughts that actually make sense with the way that the world works. The King's text is not some dull palliative. It instead breathes new consciousness into our minds, giving us the lift that we need. It is sharper than any other instrument that might work on our minds, more effective than any other tool to improve our thinking. The text introduces us to life's fullness for which the King made us. We only need to read and embrace the King's text, and then share it with those who don't know the King. We just need to *proclaim the message with intensity*, keeping his message clear, simple, and urgent, exactly as it is when communicated right.

Indeed, my inestimable brother, a deeper benefit to reading the King's text, and a real mystery, is that we become part of the King's great movement of history, part of his one great story. Alice reading a fairy tale fell into the tale, becoming its central figure. We too are so much more a product of our reading and thinking than we usually think. We are not what we eat. We do not become broccoli. Yet we become what we read. We become the image of the thoughts that we collect from the texts we encounter. When fashion consumes us, we gradually grow more coiffed and coddled like the figures that fashion forwards. When the financial pages captivate us, we spend increasing time acquiring wealth or worrying about keeping it. When we see things that promote other visions and wonders, we *don't pay any attention to what* the promoters say. They are dreamers of the wrong kind. Their dreams lead nowhere.

We know, my brother Memphis, that our beloved King embodied the full movement of history. The old part of his text said that a virgin would bear the King in Bethlehem but that we would also know him as a Nazarene. The King fulfilled that prediction when Nazarenes Mary and Joseph traveled to Bethlehem for Mary to bear the King. The King was, as the old part of his text predicted, of David's line, from the lion-tribe of Judah. At an early age, the King amazed Israel's best teachers with his insight. His brief three years of public work drew thousands whom he told that he was fulfilling the movement of history to set us free, saying, *God's Spirits is on me, he's chosen me to tell the message of good news to* set prisoners free. The King fulfilled the ancient writings so perfectly and completely that he is the good news and message more so than just carrying good news and message. He is the author of life and the full history, the *first and final, the beginning and conclusion.*

Yes, dearest friend, the King jumped from the old part's pages in full-bodied image. Yet he came to us in an image that we could understand because it was so much like us, not like some comic-book creation. His text records that he had *nothing attractive about him, nothing to cause us to take a second look.* It had to be that way that they treated him as badly as any have ever treated another, because his role was to bear their worst inclinations, to destroy those inclinations forever. And bear the he did, silently, with the incredible power and resolve that such weight would require. He *called no attention to what he did.* He just did it, and the result rang down to us in his text through millennia.

The King became the full story that the new part of his text recorded. The *Word became flesh and blood, and moved into the neighborhood.* His presence became that immediate, as familiar to us as our neighbors. That action made the text that he fulfilled much more than merely helpful instruction. That action made the King the words themselves. That action made the King's life the perfect allegory for us. We live and think allegorically, imprinting our experiences and the experiences of others over everything that we encounter in order to understand those things. The King's imprint is the perfect imprint, the perfect allegory, for us to understand and live most fully. He is so because he made the things we seek to understand. The King did much more even than his own text describes, so many things that the world is not *big enough to hold such a library* if anyone were to write them all down.

My brother, we have so full of an opportunity to join the King in his story, which is also fully our story. We can read and study the same ancient writings that he knew, allowing them to shape us into those whom the King himself intended. Yet we also have the new record of the King himself. We have full advantage of the King's life. He wants to write us into his story. We do not study the King's text to increase our lives but to share in his life, which is the greatest possible gain. If we buried our heads in the King's text while ignoring the King, then we would only harm ourselves, not help ourselves. *Here he is, standing right before us* just as his text says. We read the King's text to see and embrace him, to let our lives become living parts of his story, which is the only authentic and encompassing story.

His wish for us is that friendship honoring him for what he is. The King wants others to see him in us, so that *our lives are a letter that anyone can read just looking at us.* He writes our story in us for others to read, making us his message of love. He writes not with pen to paper but with his words affecting our minds and his Spirit influencing our hearts. We become his living text, people picking up who he is from what we say and do for them. He simultaneously makes his own record of us, like a passport into his presence. *Only those whose names he writes in his Book of Life* gets to join him. It has to be that way because of his perfection, which destroys anything outside perfection. We are glad of this closeness to him, which is better than the power it brings us. We know it is not *what we do for him but what he does for us.* When we become a part of the King's text, we get it all, the best.

To put it most simply, he is our highest reality, my brother Memphis. The atheist tells us that we imagine God. Instead, we know that the King imagines us. He writes us with the influence of his words and Spirit. The atheists *have everything backward,* telling the Maker that they make him. They don't see how silly it is to imagine anything that they made—maybe breakfast or lunch—telling them that it made them instead. While it is true that the King's words are in our minds, it is also true that we act out his words, our lives patterned that way. Our assertion that the King exists is anything but dreaming. It is instead living, which is certainly real. Let dreamers *go ahead and tell their silly dreams,* while those of us who have the King's message keep telling it like it is.

You know, the more we focus on the King, the stronger and clearer our love for others becomes. The old part of the King's text tells of an event when some relatives threw the body of a departed loved one into the tomb of one of the King's surest followers. When the body touched that followers bones, the dead loved one came right back to life. He *came alive, stood up, and walked out.* It is nothing for the King to bring a person back to life. That is how powerful his love is, more powerful than death. The King's Spirit just makes us live when we feel like we are dead. We should keep hoping and expecting that the King's Spirit makes us want to read the King's text to become more and more a part of the King's history. He gives us these rich legacies.

We should keep it simple in the end, my only brother and best friend. We aim to turn toward the King when we read the King's text. The *words that he's given us to speak, they're not going to leave our mouths.* We will just keep using those words until we reach the King. We do not make our own improvement or the improvement of those around us the reason for reading the King's text. Doing so would be to miss the main point. Instead, our aim is to get close enough to the King that we can hear him encouraging us. Sure, reading benefits us. Yes, the King instructs and expects it. But even if none of that was true, we would read for the reward of reaching the King. We *remember every road* down which the King led us toward him, knowing that we needed those roads to take the stuffing out of us so that he could get in. We needed to show him that we had the right stuff for him, which is simply the want-to for him.

What or whom do we like more than him? When we read the King's text, we show him that we care deeply for him. We want to be with him. The last part of the King's text shows these angelic beings adoring the Father on the throne in Heaven. The Father has a text. Only the Son King has the merit to take the text from the Father and read it. When the text moves from Father to Son, those angelic beings turn from Father to Son King. That turning is how powerful the text is. The *moment he took the scroll,* everyone fell down in abject submission to the King and love for the King. The King opened that Book of Life to us, my brother and friend, that text that has so much power. We follow the King because he has made this incomparable world-history text open to us. We owe it to him. No one else has given us anything close. He has earned our love, even though he gives his love to us unearned. The King's identity with the ultimate text and ultimate Being is so complete that we find the King named God and Word.

The last part of the King's text shows us our ultimate end and privilege, to be with him with an attitude that we owe him and give him everything. We would *chant night and day, never breaking,* that he was everything in the past, that he is everything presently, and that he will be everything in the future. If giving him all they've got sounds unusual or unsatisfactory to them, then they have not read the King's text correctly and understood just who he is. When they finally see him as their incredible maker, in all his magnificence, and when they have experienced just how satisfying it is to give their all for him, then they will recognize that they have no greater joy coming to them. It is like taking all of the excitement of one's youth cheering on one's favorite team or band, right in the middle of a huge crowd cheering right along, *dancing with great abandon.*

It doesn't get any better than that. Nothing we can do is such pure fun and happiness, while at the same time so right to do. The King is *on tour in the skies,* and we get to just look up and shout with all of our might at him. Everything else leaves some kind of sticky residue. Celebrating the King doesn't because he made us to do so. Nothing fits us better than honoring the King. Reading the King's text shows us just how special that end is, our purpose in which we have our one real hope of outlasting natural life to embrace perfection. It is our one hope, and it is not only possible but a given following the path we are following. By reading the King's text, we pursue the perfect life of the living King, a life he lived and recorded to pull us right up to him.

Go, my dear friend, inquiring of the King's text. Ask what the King wrote, and then act in accord with what you discover. Let him write your name in his Book of Life. Read the King's text. *They'll realize that I am their God who brought them out of the land of*

Egypt so that I could live with them. I am God, your God.

Every bit of his being told him that he had arrived, in that still-odd way that he had quickly learned soon after his arrival was the way of knowing in this eternal home. The resident knew that he had no need of looking any further. He stood at the far edge of the great field that led to the sea. His gaze took in the spectacular colors and pristine clarity of the sky, clouds, field, and sea, each seeming to shimmer with a reflection of the King's glory. Although no confusion or doubt had at any moment entered his mind since his first moment in this land, he still did not quite know the answer to the question that he had carried here with him. Now, though, he knew that the King was about to supply him with the answer, or if not the answer, then with all the encouragement that he needed.

A figure appeared at the shore of the sea, just as he had heard that it happened. The figure turned away, though, to look back across the sea out of which the figure had mysteriously arisen. He knew that whoever had emerged from the sea would need time to adjust to the glory of the land. No mind could instantly comprehend it without shattering, while the prime resident would of course have nothing within the land suffer the least of discomforts. No tear other than tears of joy would fall in this land. The figure stood solemn, gazing out across the sea.

The resident started across the great field, the brilliant golden crop parting gently at his thighs. The figure had the height, build, and, he could see as he approached closer, the hair color of his beloved brother. Yet no specific joy welled within him. He had no confirmation yet that the figure was anyone other than the next person whom the King wished him to welcome to his land. The resident had no sense whatever that the King had made anything other than the perfect judgment as to whom he should welcome. He knew that he would have no regret if the figure of his brother's similar build turned out to be someone other. Yet something within him caused him to strive through the field with a slight urgency that he had not before experienced in the land. He had not known that the King would have permitted any sense of urgency. Could it be that the King wanted him to enjoy that urgency?

As the resident approached the shore, he noticed the King standing beside the figure. The figure now looked less like the resident's brother. Indeed, the figure was not the resident's brother, the resident was now sure. The resident knew that the King's presence confirmed it. The King would in a moment address the resident's issue of his brother, the resident now also knew. The resident approached and embraced the figure, feeling again every bit of love for this new resident that the resident had felt for every other of the realm's inhabitants. He took the new resident's hand to turn him gently away from the water. The two of them started slowly across the golden plain, hand in hand, fully at ease in the expansive kingdom.

The King remained behind on the shore, facing the great sea. The resident stopped for a moment and turned back to gaze at the King. Just then, the King threw his head back and let out a roar that echoed across the water. The roar had the sound of a lion, the screech of an eagle, and the bellow of an ox. It also had the sound and meaning of the great Son of Man's voice. The resident could not repeat the precise name that the Son of Man roared across the great waters. Yet the resident understood that the Son of Man had just called once again the resident's beloved brother. The resident did not know whether his dear brother would answer. All that the resident could draw from the King's act of love was that the King knew the resident's heart for his brother.

Multitudes, multitudes
in the valley of decision!
For the day of the Lord is near
in the valley of decision.
The sun and moon will be darkened,
and the stars no longer shine.
The Lord will roar from Zion
and thunder from Jerusalem;
the earth and sky will tremble.
But the Lord will be a refuge for his people,
a stronghold for the people of Israel.

In that day the mountains will drip with new wine,
and the hills will flow with milk;
all the ravines of Judah will run with water.
A fountain will flow out of the Lord's house
and will water the valley of acacias.
But Egypt will be desolate,
*Edom a desert waste * * * .*

Joel 3:14-16, 18-19.

Epilogue

Memphis hesitated just as he started to rise from his soft chair in front of the television. Had he just heard someone call his name? No, it must have been the wind howling in the bare trees outside. He used the remote control to silence the television and paused to listen again, straining to make meaning out of the wind's howl. The effort cleared his mind, making him concentrate in a way that he had not for a long time, maybe not since his brother had died. He did not think of his brother often. They had lived apart, separated not just by distance and years but also by interest and inclination.

Now, in the howling of the wind, he recalled first his brother and then something that he could not quite grasp that was beyond his brother. That was the thing about brothers, he mused. The relationship went beyond mere goodwill into something deeper, perhaps about the spiritual connection that we have with one another. He wondered where his brother was now, this brother who had spoken of salvation and heaven. He picked up the Bible that his brother had left with him so long ago now.

The Bible fell open in his lap to a passage in which the divine figure's prayer transfigured him, clothes bright as lightning, as the divine figure talked with two long-dead prophets. The divine figure promptly returned to normal, talking and walking with his stunned disciple companions. It was such an odd book, he mused again, natural one moment but supernatural the next. He flipped to the end of the Bible, reading again of his brother's heaven, where only those lived whose names are in the book of life. He knew how one's name ended up in the book of life. One need only embrace the book's author.

He listened again to the howl of the wind. A chill ran down his spine. He did hear a name in the wind, after all. He did not hear the name "Memphis" that he knew as his own. Rather, he heard something unutterable, something that he would not repeat if he had been able. He recognized the sound as his new name. He looked outside. The trees were still, but the howl continued. He sensed in that moment, for the first time in his long life, the presence of the book's author. The author called his name. He wept in the author's howling embrace. The author wept with him.

Appendix

Italicized Quotation Citations

(All quotations taken from Eugene H. Peterson's The Message.
Copyright © 1993, 1994, 1995, 1996, 2000, 2001, 2002. Used by
permission of NavPress Publishing Group. All rights reserved.)

absolute single-heartedness — Matthew 4:10.
acquire a thorough understanding — Colossians 1:9.
add to the words or subtract from the words — Revelation 22:18.
alive, we are the King's messenger — Philippians 1:21.
an alien message, a no-message, a lie — Galatians 1:6.
another generation grew up that didn't know — Judges 2:10.
apart from faith — Hebrews 11:6.
as long as they did what they felt — Romans 6:20.
ask for directions to the old road — Jeremiah 6:16.
at that time I told them, get rid of the vile — Ezekiel 20:7.
bad business — Ecclesiastes 2:17.
bad habit of not listening — Hebrews 5:11.
banishes them to their chosen world — 2 Thessalonians 2:10.
be very careful to act exactly as — Deuteronomy 5:33.
beckoning us onward — Philippians 3:13.
bedrock under our feet — 2 Samuel 22:2.
before we saw the light of day — Jeremiah 1:5.
began telling them what was going on — Isaiah 48:4.
being up-to-date with the times — 1 Corinthians 3:18.
best by filling our minds and meditating — Philippians 4:8.
best that we were lost for a while — Philemon 15.

big enough to hold such a library — John 21:25.
bilious and bloated — Psalm 14:1.
blessed the readers — Revelation 1:3.
blessing us in all our work — Deuteronomy 16:15.
bread on the table and shoes on the feet — 1 Timothy 6:6.
break the chains of injustice — Isaiah 58:6.
breathing life on these slain bodies — Ezekiel 37:9.
brimming with knowing God-Alive — Isaiah 11:9.
brings gifts into our lives — Galatians 5:22.
brought out into the open things hidden — Matthew 13:34.
buy wisdom, buy education, buy insight — Proverbs 23:23.
called no attention to what he did — Isaiah 42:2.
came alive, stood up, and walked out — 2 Kings 13:21.
came to us, it wasn't just words — 1 Thessalonians 1:4.
can't break his word — Hebrews 6:17.
capable of knowing everything — Genesis 3:22.
case study of what he does — Colossians 1:21.
catchy opinions to tickle their fancy — 2 Timothy 4:3.
chant night and day, never breaking — Revelation 4:8.
check out everything — 1 Thessalonians 5:20.
cheerful word picks us up — Proverbs 12:25.
children, do what your parents tell you — Ephesians 6:1.
cleaned up and given a fresh start — 1 Corinthians 6:11.
cleft of the rock — Exodus 33:22.
come back, and he welcomes them — 2 Chronicles 30:9.
comes out of the mouth — Matthew 15:18.
commissioning us as judges — Psalm 82:6.
confirming the truth, the reality — 1 John 5:6.
convince parents to look after their children — Malachi 4:5.
create readiness, to nudge people toward — Matthew 13:13.
cries of the victims in Sodom and Gomorrah — Genesis 18:20.
cross-examine and test us — Psalm 139:23.
cultivate these things — 1 Timothy 4:16.
cut away the thick calluses — Deuteronomy 30:6.
dancing with great abandon — 2 Samuel 6:14.
dead men but of the living — Luke 20:38.
death's door time after time — 2 Corinthians 11:25.
delight far more about what he tells us — Psalm 119:15.
developing a rule solid and dependable — 1 Samuel 25:28.
did it out of sheer love — Deuteronomy 7:8.

die in their unclean condition — Leviticus 15:31.
die once, then face the consequences — Hebrews 9:27.
discipline your children — Proverbs 19:18.
does exactly what he promises — 1 Kings 8:23.
doesn't change—yesterday, today, tomorrow — Hebrews 13:8.
doing in us what he did in raising — Romans 10:9.
don't blame them — Acts 7:59.
don't fall for any line like that — 2 Thessalonians 2:3.
don't for a minute let this book — Joshua 1:8.
don't go against him — Exodus 23:20.
don't lay a hand on that boy — Genesis 22:12.
don't lie to one another — Colossians 3:9.
don't make me laugh — 1 Samuel 10:27.
don't pay any attention — Deuteronomy 13:1.
don't second-guess him — Proverbs 30:5.
don't try to figure out everything — Proverbs 3:5.
don't worry about what we'll say — Matthew 10:19.
doom to those who go off to Egypt — Isaiah 31:1.
dove descending, come down on him — Luke 3:21.
drag our feet — Hebrews 6:11.
drag us off into endless arguments — Colossians 2:8.
each day brimming with his beauty — Psalms 71:8.
embarrassed by their handmade gods — Jeremiah 10:14.
embarrassed over him and the way he leads — Mark 8:38.
everything connected with that way — Colossians 3:5.
everything got started in him — Colossians 1:15.
everything I once thought I had going — Philippians 3:8.
everything in between — Isaiah 44:6.
everything is clean to the clean-minded — Titus 1:15.
everything on earth is his — 1 Chronicles 29:11.
everything you need to please him — Hebrews 13:20.
examines every heart and sees through — 1 Chronicles 28:9.
Father, Son, and Holy Spirit — Matthew 28:19.
find ourselves flagging — Hebrews 12:3.
fire in our belly, a burning in our bones — Jeremiah 20:9.
fire of love stops at nothing—Song of Songs 8:7.
firm foundation under everything —Hebrews 11:1.
first and final, beginning and conclusion — Revelation 22:13.
first this: God created the Heavens — Genesis 1:1.
fixed to the rock — Matthew 7:24.

follow the road he sets out for us — Deuteronomy 10:12.
forget about what's happened — Isaiah 43:18.
formed a ring around the young king — 2 Chronicles 23:7.
found us out in the wilderness — Deuteronomy 32:10.
foundation words, words to build a life on — Luke 6:47.
friend against friend — Jeremiah 9:5.
from the first day to the last — Nehemiah 8:18.
from the waist up like burnished bronze — Ezekiel 1:26.
futility of devising some system — Galatians 3:22.
gave us his good Spirit to teach us — Nehemiah 9:20.
gentle and quiet whisper — 1 Kings 19:11.
gentle listeners and teachers who keep cool — 2 Timothy 2:25.
get them inside our children — Deuteronomy 6:6.
get us good pay — Ephesians 6:8.
gets our feet on the life path — Psalm 16:11.
gift we once had in our hands — Revelation 3:3.
give freely and spontaneously — Deuteronomy 15:10.
given to lies and changing his mind — Numbers 23:19.
gives us a map — Psalm 43:3.
go ahead and tell their silly dreams — Jeremiah 23:28.
go all out in your love for our wives — Ephesians 5:25.
go back the way we came — 1 Kings 19:15.
God look you full in the face — Numbers 6:24.
God rides on a fast-moving cloud — Isaiah 19:1.
God took us out of Egypt — Deuteronomy 26:8.
God's Spirit is on me — Luke 4:18.
going along with the crowd — Ephesians 4:17.
gone off and betrayed — Judges 10:13.
good eyes — I'm sticking with you — Jeremiah 1:12.
good life begins in the fear — Psalm 111:10.
got a good thing going — Psalm 16:8.
great ambitions for themselves — Haggai 1:8.
great success — 2 Chronicles 31:21.
guard the treasure he gave us — 1 Timothy 6:20.
gushing fountains of endless life — John 4:14.
has a whole and lasting life — John 3:17.
have everything backward — Isaiah 29:16.
hate us because of it — John 17:14.
having this bent toward evil from an early age — Genesis 8:21.
hear his voice out of Heaven — Deuteronomy 4:36.

he looked up and saw right in front of him — Joshua 5:13.
he's all we've got left — Lamentations 3:24.
heart is hopelessly dark and deceitful — Jeremiah 17:9.
here he is, standing right before us — John 5:39.
here, ready to be found — Isaiah 65:2.
here today, gone tomorrow — 2 Corinthians 4:18.
hey there, all who are thirsty — Isaiah 55:1.
him honestly and heartily — 1 Samuel 12:24.
himself present in us — 1 Corinthians 3:16.
his Spirit is in us—living and breathing — Romans 8:6.
honest with him or about him — Job 42:7.
honor our father and mother — Exodus 20:12.
hot one day, cold the next, two-faced — James 3:17.
how can mere mortals get right with God — Job 9:2.
how I wish we had an arbitrator — Job 9:33.
huge chasm set between them — Luke 16:26.
huge in mercy — Psalm 51:1.
humility, quiet strength, discipline — Colossians 3:12.
I am the road, also the truth, also the life — John 14:6.
I could go on and on — Hebrews 11:32.
I'm here, right here — Isaiah 65:2.
I'm the seer — 1 Samuel 9:17.
I've refined you, but not without fire — Isaiah 48:10.
I was in prison and you came to me — Matthew 25:36.
I'll hold the watchman responsible — Ezekiel 33:6.
I'll reduce Egypt to an empty, desolate wasteland — Ezekiel 29:9.
if you leave him, he'll leave you — 2 Chronicles 15:2.
if you warn the wicked to change — Ezekiel 33:9.
immense in mercy and with an incredible — Ephesians 2:6.
in his image — Genesis 9:6.
intelligent and good-looking — 1 Samuel 25:3.
isn't too much for us — Deuteronomy 30:11.
it's the right time to live in their fine homes — Haggai 1:4.
just one more thing—bless our families — 2 Samuel 7:28.
just what they want to do — Jeremiah 7:24.
keep the fire burning continuously — Leviticus 6:13.
keeps his commitments across — 1 Chronicles 16:15.
know how to encourage tired people — Isaiah 50:4.
know-it-alls, they know everything but — Jeremiah 8:9.
know only a portion of the truth — 1 Corinthians 13:9.

knows everything I'm going to say — Psalms 139:3.
lay out the truth to them, plain and simple — 2 Timothy 2:15.
learn the unforced rhythms of grace — Matthew 11:28.
let it fall like a gentle rain — Deuteronomy 32:1.
let the children alone — Matthew 19:14.
let us in on his plans — Exodus 33:13.
letter that anyone can read — 2 Corinthians 3:3.
life is a great mystery, far exceeding — 1 Timothy 3:16.
listen, dear friends — Psalm 78:1.
live by every word that comes from — Deuteronomy 8:3.
live carefree before — 1 Peter 5:7.
long and sorry record — Romans 3:22.
look at the way they lived — Hebrews 13:7.
look up to what is going on around — Colossians 3:2.
lose touch with reality itself — Ephesians 4:18.
lot of frantic running around, trying to figure — Daniel 12:4.
love make up for practically anything — 1 Peter 4:8.
love never gives up — 1 Corinthians 13:4.
love the King with all that's in you — Deuteronomy 6:5.
lovers of emptiness, of nothing — Isaiah 44:18.
lured away from him by the latest — Hebrews 13:9.
made a covenant between himself — 2 Chronicles 23:16.
made himself available — Isaiah 65:1.
made sure our children flourish — Genesis 22:16.
madly in love with him — Psalm 69:9.
make everything as plain as day — 1 Corinthians 13:2.
makes no difference who you are — Acts 10:34.
makes wise human insight possible — Job 32:6.
marvelous freedom of which you never — 1 Corinthians 7:22.
make a clean break of their failures — Psalm 32:5.
make you into what gives him most pleasure — Hebrews 13:21.
makes no distinction between — Ephesians 6:9.
marriage as a decision to serve the other — 1 Corinthians 7:4.
message of the Father who sent him — John 14:24.
mighty men of ancient lore, the famous ones — Genesis 6:4.
milk is for beginners — Hebrews 5:13.
minds are set on him — Isaiah 26:3.
moment he took the scroll — Revelation 5:6.
more on our side than on their side — 2 Kings 6:16.
move into the center, while we — John 3:30.

must get along with each other — 1 Corinthians 1:10.
having no idea who — Jeremiah 4:22.
mystery in a nutshell is this — Colossians 1:27.
mystery kept secret for so long — Romans 16:25.
named him the Jealous One — Exodus 34:14.
nation of ninnies, not knowing — Deuteronomy 32:28.
never get out of that bed alive — 2 Kings 1:15.
no one gets by on muscle alone — Psalm 33:17.
no small matter for us — Deuteronomy 32:47.
Noah knew that the flood was about finished — Genesis 8:6.
noble make noble plans and stand — Isaiah 32:8.
nobody's tending the store — Psalm 73:11.
not a brute strength but a glorious inner — Ephesians 3:17.
not here to demolish but to complete — Matthew 5:18.
not once have I seen an abandoned believer — Psalm 37:25.
not to demolish but to complete, to pull it all — Matthew 5:17.
nothing attractive about him — Isaiah 53:2.
now they got it and understood he reading — Nehemiah 8:12.
O holy man, have respect for my life — 2 Kings 1:13.
obeying our earthly masters — Ephesians 6:5.
oceanic, nothing gets lost — Psalm 36:5.
on our side, right alongside us — Colossians 2:2.
on tour in the skies — Psalm 19:1.
one day spent in his house — Psalm 84:10.
one we violate, and he's seen it all — Psalm 51:4.
only one foundation, the one already laid — 1 Corinthians 3:12.
only the high priest enters — Hebrews 9:7.
only those whose names he writes — Revelation 21:27.
our job is to speak out on the things — Titus 2:1.
our lives are a letter that anyone can read — 2 Corinthians 3:2.
our lives gradually becoming brighter — 2 Corinthians 3:18.
pass it off as just one more opinion — 1 Thessalonians 2:13.
pass on his counsel — 1 Timothy 4:6.
peaceful repose better than fistfuls — Ecclesiastes 4:6.
people who try other ways — Isaiah 8:20.
personally, to experience his resurrection — Philippians 3:10.
picked us out as his — 2 Thessalonians 2:13.
plan on looking him full in the face — Psalm 17:15.
plans to give us the future — Jeremiah 29:11.
pour it out to the King — Psalm 45:1.

pour pure water over us and scrub us clean — Ezekiel 36:26.
proclaim the message with intensity — 2 Timothy 4:2.
put a snake on a flagpole — Numbers 21:8.
quickly tired of him — Isaiah 43:22.
raising the roof — Psalm 32:11.
read between the lines — 2 Corinthians 1:13.
refuse to obey the message — 2 Thessalonians 1:8.
religious sales talk — Ephesians 5:7.
remember every road — Deuteronomy 8:2.
reminds us of all the things — John 14:26.
reputation for vigor but stone dead — Revelation 3:1.
revelation is whole — Psalm 19:7.
reverently responsive to what he says — Isaiah 66:2.
richly embroidered coat — Genesis 37:3.
right there with us, fighting — Deuteronomy 20:4.
road stretches straight and true — Psalm 18:30.
rock whose works are perfect — Deuteronomy 32:4.
run for your life from all this — 1 Timothy 6:12.
says goes and stays as permanent — Psalm 119:89.
says what he means — 1 Samuel 15:29.
seed sown is natural — 1 Corinthians 15:42.
self-absorbed, money-hungry — 2 Timothy 3:1.
sending the misdirected in the right direction — Psalm 25:9.
set in their ways, they won't change — Psalm 55:19.
set it all out before us — Ephesians 1:8.
set ourselves apart — Leviticus 20:7.
settled on us as the focus of his love — Ephesians 1:4.
shaped us first inside then out — Psalm 139:13.
shaped us in the womb — Jeremiah 1:5.
sharp edge of their expectation dulled — Luke 21:34.
she came to put his reputation to the test — 1 Kings 10:1.
sheer silliness for those hellbent — 1 Corinthians 1:18.
show up empty-handed — Deuteronomy 16:17.
showing up in the good things we do — Philemon 6.
simple and straightforward — Colossians 2:6.
sledgehammer busting a rock — Jeremiah 23:29.
slink along Dead-End Road — Psalm 1:1.
smashing warped philosophies — 2 Corinthians 10:5.
smeared with filth inside and out — Romans 1:24.
so let's get moving and build — 1 Chronicles 22:19.

some people are blatant — 1 Timothy 5:24.
sons of light and daughters of day — 1 Thessalonians 5:5.
Spirit of Truth to take us by the hand — John 16:13.
stand in faith or you won't have a leg — Isaiah 7:9.
starting from scratch, he made the entire race — Acts 17:26.
stay at our post reading — 1 Timothy 4:13.
stayed calm, minded their own — 1 Thessalonians 4:11.
stay silent at a time like this — Esther 4:14.
stay strong and steady — Joshua 23:6.
stay where we were when — 1 Corinthians 7:20.
steady, constant calling and warm personal — Romans 15:4.
stick with what we learned — 2 Timothy 3:14.
sticks by those who stick with him — 2 Samuel 22:26.
strip down, start running, and never quit — Hebrews 12:1.
study how he did it — Hebrews 12:2.
subjected themselves again to paper tigers — Galatians 4:9.
swept in ecstasy to the heights — 2 Corinthians 12:2.
take a good look at the way we are living — Lamentations 3:40.
take all the help we can get — Ephesians 6:14.
take care of the hidden things — Deuteronomy 29:29.
take in the extravagant dimensions—Ephesians 3:17.
takes a steady stream of words — Matthew 4:4.
taking a long and thoughtful look — Romans 1:20.
talked about all the things she cared about — 1 Kings 10:2.
the King, the only King there is — Isaiah 45:5.
the tree looked like good eating — Genesis 3:17.
the way I think is beyond the way you think — Isaiah 55:8.
the word was first — John 1:1.
there's no one without it — 2 Chronicles 6:36.
there is no difference between us and them — Romans 3:22.
they'll realize that I am their God — Exodus 29:46.
things he wants us to teach — 1 Timothy 6:2.
those who work in the Temple live off — 1 Corinthians 9:13.
thundering breakers crash and crush us — Psalm 42:7.
translated so they could understand it — Nehemiah 8:8.
trivialize our holy work — Ezekiel 44:19.
truth will free us — John 8:32.
turn our language into babble — Genesis 11:8.
turns out well — 1 Samuel 18:14.
understanding what they're reading—Acts 8:30.

unsuspecting souls they can bedevil — Matthew 12:43.
upstart apostles were instructing the people — Acts 4:1.
useful one way or another — 2 Timothy 3:16.
useless for either good or evil - Jeremiah 10:8.
useless to rise early — Psalm 127:2.
validate our lives in the clear light of day — Psalm 37:5.
wake up, you sleepyhead people — Psalm 24:7.
walk in darkness and to see a great light — Isaiah 9:2.
wanted nothing to do with its God — 1 Samuel 10:18.
wasn't so long ago that we ourselves — Titus 3:3.
watch out for doomsday deceivers — Matthew 24:6.
watch your standard of living going up — Deuteronomy 8:12.
water no one could walk through — Ezekiel 47:5.
water pouring out from the temple — Ezekiel 47:1.
way off base and here's why — Mark 12:24.
we all die sometime — 2 Samuel 14:14.
we did all this — Deuteronomy 8:17.
we wanted to talk, but they were always — Matthew 11:17.
we warn people not to add to his message — Colossians 1:28.
what good is a birthright if I'm dead — Genesis 25:32.
what he says goes — Hebrews 4:12.
what we do for him but what he does for us — Luke 10:20.
whatever they want to do — Galatians 5:13.
when I walked downtown and sat — Job 29:7.
while he's here to be found — Isaiah 55:6.
why should the work come to a standstill — Nehemiah 6:3.
will break their strong pride — Leviticus 26:19.
winter coat, books, and notebooks — 2 Timothy 4:13.
without him, nothing makes sense — Psalm 16:2.
wolf romps with the lamb — Isaiah 11:6.
wondrously powerful and transforming — Romans 15:18.
Word became flesh and blood — John 1:14.
word we can take to heart and depend on — 1 Timothy 1:15.
words are pure words, refined — Psalm 12:6.
words that he's given us to speak — Isaiah 59:21.
work from the heart for our real master — Colossians 3:23.
work heartily as his servants — Ephesians 6:7.
worked together at their common trade — Acts 18:2.
worked up about what may or may not — Matthew 6:34.
worked up over nothing — Luke 10:40.

world doesn't know the first thing — Ephesians 2:1.
wrong since before we were born — Psalm 51:5.
you gave bread from heaven — Nehemiah 9:15.
you wouldn't understand — it's sheer wonder — Judges 13:18.
you're blessed when you are at the end — Matthew 5:3.
your body a sacred place — 1 Corinthians 6:19.
your famous and righteous ways — Psalm 71:19.
your love will flourish and you will — Philippians 1:9.